She knew she was already in too deep, knew that there was nothing she could do to turn off her traitorous emotions.

He angled her head for a kiss. Her pregnant belly was firm and spooned right into his stomach as though their bodies were made to fit that way....

The sound of her moan was lost in his mouth as his lips finally closed over hers. His kiss was sure and strong, yet soft and seductive. The joy he created with just that touch was potent, liberating. She wanted to take it further, to press closer, skin to skin—

The porch light winked on and off. She jumped, pulled back for an instant and once more met the heat of his eyes.

Flynn gave a strained laugh. "Been a while since I've worried about being caught necking on a girl's front porch," he said.

The explosion of emotions that burst through him took him by surprise. Darcie Moretti was no shrinking violet when it came to giving and taking...or kissing. She didn't play games or wait for him to lead. She participated, gave it her all. And man alive! What that "all" did to him.

Dear Reader,

Welcome to another month of wonderful books from Harlequin American Romance! We've rounded up the best stories by your favorite authors, with the hope that you will enjoy reading them as much as we enjoy bringing them to you.

Kick-start a relaxing weekend with the continuation of our fabulous miniseries, THE DADDY CLUB. The hero of Mindy Neff's *A Pregnancy and a Proposal* is one romantic daddy who knows how to sweep a woman off her feet!

Beloved historical author Millie Criswell makes her contemporary romance debut with *The Wedding Planner*. We are thrilled to bring you this compelling story of a wealthy bachelor out to find himself a bride...with a little help from the wedding consultant who wishes she were his only choice!

We've also got the best surprises and secrets. Bailey Dixon has a double surprise for Michael Wade in Tina Leonard's delightful new Western, *Cowboy Be Mine*. And in Bonnie K. Winn's *The Mommy Makeover*, a dedicated career woman is suddenly longing for marriage—what *is* her handsome groom's secret?

With best wishes for happy reading from Harlequin American Romance...

Melissa Jeglinski
Associate Senior Editor

A Pregnancy and a Proposal

MINDY NEFF

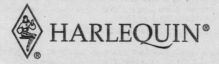

HARLEQUIN®

TORONTO • NEW YORK • LONDON
AMSTERDAM • PARIS • SYDNEY • HAMBURG
STOCKHOLM • ATHENS • TOKYO • MILAN • MADRID
PRAGUE • WARSAW • BUDAPEST • AUCKLAND

To Louise Weaver,
From girlhood to womanhood, through slumber parties
and heart valves and babies and weddings—
we've survived it all.
Thanks, girlfriend…and Happy Birthday!

ISBN 0-373-16809-8

A PREGNANCY AND A PROPOSAL

Copyright © 2000 by Melinda Neff.

Visit us at www.romance.net

Printed in U.S.A.

ABOUT THE AUTHOR

Originally from Louisiana, Mindy Neff settled in Southern California where she married a really romantic guy and raised five great kids. Family, friends, writing and reading are her passions. When not writing, Mindy's ideal getaway is a good book, hot sunshine and a chair at the river's edge with water lapping at her toes.

Mindy loves to hear from readers and can be reached at P.O. Box 2704-262, Huntington Beach, CA 92647.

Books by Mindy Neff

HARLEQUIN AMERICAN ROMANCE

644—A FAMILY MAN
663—ADAM'S KISS
679—THE BAD BOY NEXT DOOR
711—THEY'RE THE ONE!
739—A BACHELOR FOR THE BRIDE
759—THE COWBOY IS A DADDY
769—SUDDENLY A DADDY
795—THE VIRGIN & HER BODYGUARD*
800—THE PLAYBOY & THE MOMMY*
809—A PREGNANCY AND A PROPOSAL

*Tall, Dark & Irresistible

THE **DADDY** CLUB

Upcoming topics

Week 1: Romantic Dinners for 2...or 3...or 4...
Meals to woo a woman when your
kids are dining

Week 2: Top Ten Tips on Teens
How to avoid the minefields in your
house and give peace a chance

Week 3: Potty Training: It's not for the weak!

Week 4: "You're going to be a daddy...again!"
How to survive—and thrive on—
fatherhood, the second time around

Be there...
for vital information for every single father!

Chapter One

During the last five months, Flynn O'Grady had visualized countless scenarios of meeting Darcie Moretti again. Never in his wildest dreams had he imagined that in the middle of a Daddy Club meeting, he would look up and see her walking toward him.

His heart pounded a fierce tattoo in his chest at the sight of her. Her hair was a mass of messy brown curls that she'd corralled with two barrettes and a couple of chopsticks. Millions of golden freckles dusted her skin, fascinating him.

Darcie Moretti had a way of looking at a man that made him feel aggressive and startled and special and primitive all at once. She didn't shy away; her gaze didn't skitter coyly.

So why had she disappeared on him that night at the hotel? He had so many questions. Where had she been? Why had she left him without even saying goodbye, without giving him a phone number? And—

"Your daughter just called the runaway hot line."

She was standing in front of him now, those quick-to-smile, clever lips set in a grim line.

"Did you hear what I said, Flynn?"

"Yes, I—" His brain finally absorbed the full impact of her words. He uncrossed his legs. His foot dropped to the floor. His body tightened, poised in that split instant of fight or flight, as though the folding chair had just collapsed beneath him, as though his world were collapsing, as well.

He felt the blood drain from his face, forgot that six single fathers were sitting in a semicircle around him at the Hardware and Muffins store in Princeton, each of them part of a Wednesday-night school for hapless fathers. "What did you say?"

"Heather's planning to run away…if she hasn't already."

He leaped to his feet, never thinking to ask how she knew his daughter, or even where she would get such a ludicrous idea. They'd slept together once, on a sultry, late-summer evening when he'd been drowning his woes in a bottle of whiskey. She'd been like a breath of fresh air that night, a balm to his bruised soul.

But he didn't recall mentioning his family.

"She can't run away! I just saw her thirty minutes ago. At home. I haven't been gone long enough." Fear and disbelief battered him at once. Was there no end to the nightmares a parent could suffer? Horrible thoughts crossed his mind of what could happen to his little girl out on the streets. Never mind that the Princeton suburb they lived in was touted as one of the safest places in New Jersey. A young girl could make poor choices. Hell, she could slip on the ice and be buried under a foot of snow in less than an hour.

Darcie automatically reached out and placed a hand on Flynn's arm. She saw his skin pale with genuine distress, and like always, she responded to that distress. She shouldn't. God knows she'd gotten herself in plenty of trouble with her soft heart—a prime case in point was that night five months ago in a Philadelphia hotel room.

But darn it all, this man needed help.

When Heather O'Grady had called the runaway hot line where Darcie volunteered, Darcie had nearly had a stroke. She'd told herself every morning for the last three months that she should and *would* contact Flynn O'Grady. And every morning she'd chickened out.

His daughter, in a wild twist of fate, had settled the dilemma—and presented a whole new one. One that nearly ripped Darcie's heart in two.

"Where did she go?" Flynn asked. "Did she say where she was going? What did she say?" The questions were fired one right after the other. "Is she still at home?"

"I doubt it," Darcie said, hating the crestfallen look on his face.

"I've got to find her, call the cops…"

She shouldn't get involved, should turn this case over to someone else. But that mushy heart of hers was already crying out its intentions. Not only were those intentions going to be dangerous, they were likely going to cause her great heartache. She'd felt the chemistry moments ago—right before she'd dropped her bombshell. In just a split second of eye contact, she felt him draw her in with those watch-out-woman bedroom eyes and knew he'd been re-membering their night together. And her body had reacted to that sexual pull in a giddy flutter of hor-mones...in an exquisite, bittersweet wash of remem-brance.

She wanted to just stand there and stare, to soak up every nuance of his *GQ* model looks, his scent, the way the white shirt rode his broad shoulders and the silk tie hung from his neck, the way the belt circled his trim waist, his pants draping and kissing his lean hips...

Well, honestly, Darcie, just stop it!

She reached for his arm again, stopping him from charging out of the store.

"I know a little about the way the police depart-ment works, and you're not going to make headway at this early stage of the game."

"Early? She's thirteen years old and she just said she was going to run away!" He pinned her with a look. "And why did she tell *you?* How do you know my daughter?"

"I volunteer for a runaway hot line here in town." Her hand tightened on his arm. He looked like he was going to pass out. She eased up against him, bolstered him with her body.

Oh, no, she nearly groaned. *Bad move.* The feel of his warm body pressed against her sent her hor-mones right off the charts. He needed her help. Not her fantasies.

The way he was looking at her made her squirm. Flynn O'Grady was a sexy mixture of worry, confusion and questions. She understood his worry, sympathized with his confusion and feared his questions.

"Are you okay?" she asked, easing a fraction of an inch away, still watching him in case he did indeed faint.

"No, I'm not. I've got to find my daughter." He shoved his arms through his coat as he headed for the door. Then he stopped as though he'd forgotten something vital.

"The baby," he muttered, and changed direction, striding toward Ruth Naomi Steadwell, the owner of Hardware and Muffins. The Daddy Club participants gave him room. Panic and determination radiated from him. He hitched a diaper bag over his shoulder, scooped Mary Beth into his arms and gave Ruth Naomi a distracted thank-you.

Darcie watched all this, her emotions reeling once more. She'd known he had children. If you wanted to learn anything about anybody, Ula Mae Simmons—one of the KoffeeKlatch regulars—would happily tell you. Still, seeing him with one-year-old Mary Beth in his arms jolted her.

Reining in the emotions, she barely stopped herself from shaking her head. He was like a bull charging blindly. His heart and intentions were in the right place, but he was very likely going to screw up royally. She didn't want to see that happen.

Darcie stepped in his path. "Flynn, wait."

He seemed confused, surprised that she was there.

"Do you know where my daughter is? Where I can look?"

"I have an idea."

"Then tell me."

Now this was the tricky part. She couldn't quite hold his gaze. "Um...I can't."

His chocolate eyes went from delicious warmth to black fire in an instant. "What do you mean, you can't?"

"What the hot line personnel talk about with the kids is confidential."

"Conf—" His expression incredulous, he didn't seem able to finish the word.

And Darcie didn't seem able to think—an odd occurrence given that she was normally a sharp, witty woman. Her cheeks felt overheated and her heart pounded as though someone had injected her with an ampoule of adrenaline.

Oh, no. She recognized this feeling. It had been happening to her with some regularity in the past four months and it meant that she was very close to experiencing one of those weird spells.

And the very last thing she wanted to do was crumple into a heap at Flynn O'Grady's feet.

Whirling, she made a beeline for the rest room.

Flynn watched as Darcie Moretti disappeared through an inner sanctuary where men normally didn't trod. It took him a full moment to realize that she'd bailed on him. Again!

This wasn't acceptable. The clock was ticking. His daughter was in the process of running away to God only knew where.

And the woman who held the answers had apparently thought to escape him by hiding out in the ladies' rest room.

Well, by damn, she'd underestimated him. He was a man on a thin string. A harried father. No gender sign on a pressboard swinging door would stop him.

Hitching Mary Beth higher on his hip, he slammed his hand against the door and pushed it open. From behind him, he heard approving noises from The Daddy Club guys, and an indrawn breath or two from the older patrons watching from the designer coffee bar in the back of the hardware store.

He ignored it all, allowed the door to swing closed behind him, sealing them away from prying eyes and ears. He focused his attention on the startled, freckle-faced woman staring at him with her back up against the salmon tiled vanity, her dripping wet fingers fiddling with the shiny black buttons on her baggy coat.

Frowning, he noticed that her pale face was also wet. "Are you okay?"

"Fine."

Her tone wasn't all that convincing but he let it go. "Look, Darcie, if you've got information about my daughter, I expect you to give it over." It was tough to look menacing and serious with mushy animal crackers decorating his shirt, a squirming baby on his hip and a pink cloth diaper bag slung over his shoulder.

But he gave it a good shot, despite the fact that desperation was climbing and his imagination of what could happen to his daughter was vivid and ugly, sending him into near panic.

One of Darcie's golden brows arched and her hazel eyes took on a look of censure. She reached for a paper towel and dried her face and hands. "Do you threaten your daughter like that?"

"I'm *not* threatening—" Appalled, offended, he broke off, tried to gather his wits. Was it the situation or the woman who had him so scattered, so close to the boiling point? It annoyed him that she'd left him, asleep and naked, five months ago. And it annoyed him that she'd just popped up in his life again. All that annoyance was getting tangled up in his panic over Heather. "No, I do not threaten my daughter!"

The baby winced, blinked. Her lip trembled.

"Now look what you've done," Darcie said. She reached out and plucked Mary Beth out of his arms.

"Wait just a—"

"Hush."

Flynn didn't know if she'd meant the baby or him, but he was surprised enough to obey. He didn't normally hand his kid over to just anybody. Actually, he hadn't really handed her, Darcie had taken her and he hadn't put up a fight.

He nearly groaned. What kind of a father was he? He couldn't even hold on to his baby daughter. Could just any old stranger pluck his baby out of his arms?

And what about Heather? She was lost. *He'd* lost her.

How had that happened? Why hadn't he known she was that unhappy?

He should have seen it—especially tonight. He'd asked her to baby-sit Mary Beth so he could come to this Daddy Club meeting, but she'd thrown a hissy fit. Frustrated, he'd snatched up Mary Beth and stormed out of the house.

Oh, man. He was such an idiot.

"Hey, it'll be all right."

He felt Darcie's hand on his arm, met her compassionate eyes, noticed that the color had come back into her cheeks.

Mary Beth was happily twisting messy fingers in Darcie's curly hair, dislodging several unruly strands from its sexy updo. Darcie didn't seem to notice or to mind. And for some confounded reason, that touched him.

"I'm at a disadvantage here. You seem to have all the answers—about my daughter…and about where you've been for the past five months, why you left…"

His words trailed off, inviting her to pick up the conversational ball. He knew the timing of personal questions was inappropriate, but he felt like an ostrich looking for a hole in the sand to bury his head. Maybe if he stalled long enough, somebody would burst through the door and tell him it was all a mistake, that his daughter was home, safe and sound and happy, and that he wasn't failing miserably at just about everything he did lately.

"I don't have all the answers, Flynn." She shifted the baby so that Mary Beth's diaper-clad bottom was perched on the shelf of her arm. The baby laid her head on Darcie's shoulder, and something in Flynn's chest tightened. It didn't make sense, but just that simple move made him feel inadequate. That was an emotion he was becoming increasingly familiar with these days.

"As for me," she said. "I haven't been hiding."

"I thought you lived in Philly."

"Did I say that?"

"No. You didn't say much of anything."

"You'd had a lot to drink." She smiled. "Maybe we should start over." She held out her hand. "Darcie Moretti, physical address Trenton, New Jersey. Same town I've lived in all my life."

Flynn felt ridiculous exchanging pleasantries in the women's rest room—especially in light of the fact that they'd slept together—but somehow Darcie Moretti made it seem normal.

He accepted her hand, felt a kinetic jolt that both shocked and worried him. He saw her hazel eyes widen, saw them darken to the color of moss.

"Well," she murmured. "This is awkward."

His laughter was both strained and spontaneous—and took him totally by surprise. "You're a contradiction, Darcie Moretti. You pull a feminine stunt by hiding out in the rest room, then blatantly admit to an attraction."

"I didn't blatantly admit to an attraction. I only made a comment."

"An admission," he argued. "And along those lines, how about some straight talk about where you think my daughter took off to."

Her gaze didn't skitter this time. It held his. "I'd rather not say."

"And I'd rather that you did. We're standing in the women's rest room, for crying out loud. We've gone to bed together. If that doesn't invite confidences, I don't know what does." Now her gaze did jerk away, making him think of avoidance and secrets. First things first, he reminded himself. Find Heather, and *then* get the whole story on Darcie Moretti and her disappearing acts.

"Tell me, Darcie."

She shook her head. "I'm only as good as my word. I work at the hot line and promise the kids who call me that they're safe talking to me. If I betrayed that confidence, word would get around on the street. Kids would stop calling and they'd end up in bad situations and it would be my fault."

Something raw and painful shimmered in her tone, but he told himself to let it go. "I'm not going to spread rumors. We're talking about my *daughter*."

"She may be your daughter, but she called me."

He felt his frustration rising, tried to tamp it back down. "I'm not such a bad guy. I don't beat her. I try to give her everything I can."

"Except your time?"

"Did she say that?"

"Sometimes she does."

"Sometimes she does?" he repeated. "She's called you more than once?"

"Yes. I've been talking to her for about three weeks. Since just before New Year's Eve."

Flynn raked a hand through his hair, dislodged a hunk of sticky animal cracker, and wiped his hand on his coat, uncaring that it left a light brown smear.

''We had a fight New Year's Eve. She wanted to go to a party and I said no. I didn't know she was still mad about that.'' He heaved a sigh and focused on her reflection in the mirror, noticing that one of the chopsticks shoved haphazardly in her curly hair was slipping.

''According to Heather you claimed it was family night, but a friend came over and Heather ended up baby-sitting Mary Beth while you ignored both of the girls and had drinks with the other woman.''

His gaze jerked back to her face. If he hadn't known better, he'd have sworn Darcie Moretti's tone was laced with jealousy.

''I did not ignore her, and I didn't make her baby-sit! I was home. And that other woman was Ross Steadwell's wife, Elaine! Ross was there, too, and so were their kids.''

''Oh.'' She didn't look a bit contrite over her show of jealousy—if it had even been that. ''Aren't Ariel and Jimmy cuties?''

''You know them?''

''Very well. I handle the insurance for Data Ink. where Elaine works. In fact, uh…I'm the one who suggested that she and Ross get you involved in The Daddy Club.''

She seemed almost apologetic. Still, Flynn didn't like people going behind his back, orchestrating his life. Never mind that his life seemed to be out of control lately and he could probably use some coaching. He still didn't like it.

"Does Heather think I'm that bad?"

"No. She's just a confused young girl."

"What about me? I'm confused, too. I'm trying my best, but it doesn't seem to be good enough. Look at me. I'm a mess. I've got animal crackers and baby slobber all over me. I nearly charged out of Hardware and Muffins without my baby. My other daughter is mad enough at me to run away and I don't know why! And you claim to have answers that you won't give."

"I can't betray Heather's confidence, Flynn."

The roiling in his gut was so powerful, he thought he might explode. Or cry. When she reached out to touch him, he jerked back. He didn't know which emotion would rule, and he couldn't chance letting her accidentally push him over the edge.

The woman was stubborn, but she smelled of apples and cinnamon and radiated compassion and capability. She made him think of home and hearth and family—all the things he wanted most. She made him think of intimacy and fun also, two things that had been sorely lacking from his life for quite a while now.

Or at least since that night five months ago.

Even though he'd had more to drink than he should have, he remembered it clearly. Remembered Darcie clearly, her passion, her verve, her whole-hearted giving.

Right now, though, she wasn't willing to give. She held the key to his daughter's whereabouts.

How could he make her understand how torn up and frightened he felt at the thought of something happening to his daughter?

"Heather's had it rough this past year. Her mom left right after Mary Beth was born, then ended up getting killed in an accident. My mom moved in with us, which really helped the girls over the hump, but she recently had to leave for Vermont to take care of my aunt who had hip surgery—and I don't know why I'm telling you all this." Saying it out loud made him realize how many women in his life had abandoned him. Some intentionally, some not so intentionally. God, he'd failed as a husband, and now his incompetence had him failing as a dad.

He was the one who'd wanted so desperately to be a father…but he hadn't dreamed he'd have to do it as a full-time, *single* parent.

And failing dismally after the first three weeks of being on his own.

"You've got no reason to trust me, Flynn, but will you?" she asked softly.

"Trust you how?"

"Let me go find Heather."

"I can't…. That's my job."

"You're going to stand on what you think is *expected* of you in a situation like this?" She shook her head, heaved in a breath. "As her parent you can force her to come home, but you can make it worse, too. And what's to say she'll stay put? She's gotten up the nerve to make a move. The next time it won't be as hard. Are you going to stay up all night watching her to make sure she doesn't run again?''

"If I have to." He'd do whatever it took, stick to her like glue, quit his job, rent a secluded cabin in the Pocono Mountains and force her to... To what? he wondered.

"I'm trying to tell you it might not be necessary. You need a mediator."

"And you think that's you?"

"I'm the one she's been talking to. I'm the one she seems to trust right now." She stroked the curls at the back of Mary Beth's head, absently pressed a kiss to the baby's hair. "Heather's had a lot of upsets in her world lately."

"I don't need you to tell me the sorry happenings in my life," he said tightly.

"See there?"

"What?"

"You're not in the right frame of mind to successfully deal with Heather right now."

Resentment made him edgy and sharp. "Don't tell me how to deal with my—''

"Hold it right there, buddy." Darcie jiggled and soothed when Mary Beth looked like she was going to cloud up again over the squabbling. "I'm trying not to judge you. I'm trying to help Heather. I'm trying to help *you*. *I* didn't tell your daughter to run away—or to call me, for that matter. But she has and she did. I'm involved whether you like it or not. And because I'm an outside party, I can be more objective. If you go blazing after her, your emotions are going to come across as anger and you're going to make it worse. Trust me, I know what I'm talking about.''

Her impassioned words seemed to echo off the tiled walls of the rest room. For a long moment, Flynn didn't comment. He just watched her, making her squirm, making her forget why they were there...making her want.

"Did you run away?" His voice was soft and deep.

"No, but a close friend in school did." Darcie didn't want to think about that outcome. But her heart clenched anyway. "And we're wasting precious time." She juggled the baby as she reached for a piece of paper.

"Here, let me take Mary Beth."

Darcie kissed the baby's cheek and passed her back to Flynn, deliberately ignoring the flash of heat that streaked up her arms as their hands bumped and tangled.

Why, oh, why did she have to be so crazy about this guy?

With fingers that trembled slightly, she wrote down the address and telephone number of her parents' house and handed it to Flynn.

"This is where my folks live. Are you familiar with the area?" The address was in a blue-collar section of Trenton called the burg. Her family had lived there for more than thirty years. At one time Flynn O'Grady had too.

"I can find it," Flynn said.

"Good. Give me an hour head start and then meet me there."

"I don't like this."

She softened, placed her hand on his arm and gave a compassionate squeeze. The jolt was there, as she'd expected. But she couldn't *not* touch him. This man needed. Needed badly.

And that's why she'd suggested her family's home to meet. If she had any hope of staying out of trouble with him, she needed people around her.

Added to that, her mother had plenty of experience soothing the ruffled feathers of a rebellious teen. It was a knack. Between her mother and her grandmother, they would *feed* Heather back into good humor. And if Darcie's guess was right, Flynn would come away from the evening a winner, too. Nobody left the Moretti house without a meal or dessert or a week's worth of leftovers.

"I know you don't like it, Flynn," she said softly, making herself remove her hand after one final squeeze—that one purely for herself. "But please let me try with her first. I want the best for all of you."

He nodded, his nicely tapered fingers absently stroking his baby daughter's silky blond curls. "I'll meet you in an hour."

She hoped to God that was long enough.

And she hoped she'd find the nerve somewhere along the way to tell him he was going to be a daddy. Again.

Chapter Two

Heather O'Grady sniffed and wrapped her gloved hands around the chain of the swing, pushing off with her feet. The canvas strip hugged her thighs like a soft horseshoe cradle as the metal chains creaked against the swing set crossbar. It was dark in the playground, and quiet.

Snow started to fall again, the flakes dropping and melting against her coat. Absently she wondered if they would pile up in her lap if she stayed real still. Would they freeze her to death? Would anybody find her frozen body? A kid, maybe?

Oh, that wouldn't be right.

Heather thought about her baby sister, Mary Beth. She was a cute kid, and Heather loved her. But sometimes she sort of resented her, too. If Mary Beth weren't around, Mom would probably still be here.

The minute the thought surfaced, she pushed it back. She wasn't quick enough to stop the sting of tears, though, the horrible ache in her throat. Her breath puffed out in a cloud as a soft sob escaped.

This park had been her playground, the place where she and Mom had come, just the two of them. Before Mom had gotten that stupid job. Before the baby was born.

Heather swiped at her cheeks, her gloves scratching her wind-chapped face. It wasn't fair to blame the baby. She pictured Mary Beth's cute little face, her round blue eyes, the way her dark blond hair flipped up around her tiny ears. The kid slobbered a lot, but that was probably because she was getting more teeth.

Pride nudged her. She was getting good at guessing what was wrong with Mary Beth, tending to the baby's needs. Sometimes, she even felt sort of like a mom, which was a pretty weird feeling for a thirteen-year-old girl to have.

She felt old one minute and young the next. She wanted to be a little kid again, then five minutes later she wanted to drive and go to parties and hang out alone with Robbie Sanders. She'd been thinking about sex lately and that made her feel really confused—and guilty. Robbie wanted to do it and she kept saying no. Her friend Gina Warnelli said it was no big deal, that she should just go ahead and do it. But Gina had a bad reputation, and Heather didn't want everybody talking about her that way.

She couldn't admit to any of her friends that she didn't really know anything about sex. They'd think she was some kind of prehistoric creature or something. But who was she supposed to ask? Not her dad. He'd blow a gasket. He'd immediately assume she was talking about Robbie, and he'd do something stupid, like taking the phone away or grounding her till she was thirty or something. Her dad already thought Robbie was too old—just because he was in high school! That was so stupid. It wasn't like she was a baby or anything.

She kicked at the sand where glistening snowflakes turned the earth damp. Her heart lurched when she saw a shadow from the corner of her eye. Her fingers tightened against the chain. What if some bad guys tried to come and take her?

A whimper sneaked past her throat, catching her off guard, scaring her half to death. Then she really *did* feel like a baby. Nobody was there…were they? Her eyes burned from staring and her palms stung where the chain cut into them through her wool gloves.

Maybe she should go find a phone and call Robbie. Or maybe she should just go home. She'd told Darcie Moretti she was gonna run away, but so what? Darcie only knew her name, not what she looked like or anything. It wasn't like she'd have to face the lady or anything. And Dad didn't know she was gone. He was at that stupid Daddy Club meeting trying to figure out how to be a Mr. Mom.

She rolled her eyes. If only he'd just get a clue.

Headlights swept the playground equipment as a compact car pulled to the curb. Heather's heart pumped.

Daddy?

Relief swept her and she nearly cried out. Then she took a closer look, her heart dropping like a stone.

It wasn't Daddy. The car was too small and there wasn't a baby seat in the back.

And Daddy was totally oblivious to what she was doing anyway. Like that was any big news flash, she thought.

As whoever it was got out of the car Heather picked up a rock and cupped her gloved fingers around it. She was scared. She was sorry she'd come out here. She was cold.

Tears burned her throat, swam in her eyes. It seemed like all she did lately was cry. How many tears did a girl have, anyway? The problem was, she didn't even know why she hurt this way. Her insides stung, felt like they were churning, like if she just opened her mouth, all the bad thoughts would bubble up and come out in a loud scream.

Her fingers tightened around the rock. The person wasn't so big. And Heather was pretty tall for thirteen. Already five foot five. It gave her an advantage, made people think she was older. Daddy didn't like that. But so what? Why should he care anyway? He was always so busy, always had those blueprints spread out on his worktable and his head bent over them, always expected Grandma or her to take care of Mary Beth.

Shoot, *she* was only thirteen, yet he never bothered to wonder who would take care of *her,* did he?

Her eyes squinted and her heart still raced. It was hard to tell if the figure approaching was a man or woman.

''Heather?'' The voice was female. ''Heather, it's Darcie Moretti from the hot line.''

As Darcie came closer, her coat flapped open and the wind plastered her top against her. Heather stared. She thought the lady was fat. But the lady wasn't fat.

She was pregnant.

Heather's heart sank. For some reason, pregnant ladies bugged her. Seeing them made her feel bad inside. Her mom had been pregnant and then she'd left.

"May I sit with you?"

Heather shrugged. "I guess." She watched, intrigued by the way the sling style swing seat molded to Darcie's hips, by the way Darcie's pregnant belly pooched out and rested in her lap. "Does that hurt you?"

Confused, Darcie frowned. Then she noticed the direction of Heather's gaze. Guilt made her grab at her coat, tug it around her. Of all times to let down her guard—and of all people to let it down in front of! "What? The baby?"

Heather nodded.

"No, only when she's pretending to be a basketball star. That can get a little tricky. Thank goodness she's still small yet."

"A she? How do you know?"

"I had a sonogram."

"Oh." Heather jutted out her chin and looked away. "I didn't know you were pregnant."

"No, I suppose it never came up. Little reason it should. Is that a problem?"

Heather shrugged and kicked at the sand. "I told

you stuff about me. You could have told me stuff about you.''

''Is that what you'd like?''

''Doesn't make no difference.''

Darcie skimmed her fingers over Heather's hair. This young girl was a fraud, trying to act all tough, when she was scared silly and aching for attention. Darcie had seen this same attitude on so many adolescent faces. She'd worn it herself as a teen.

''You know, kiddo, I wouldn't go back to being your age for all the money in the world.''

Heather's eyes filled and Darcie slid off the swing, sank to her knees in front of her and gathered the young girl in her arms. ''Oh, honey, it's okay. It's all going to work out.'' *Please God, let it all work out.*

''No, it's not.'' Heather sniffed. ''I hate him. He treats me like a baby one minute and then wants me to do grown-up stuff the next.''

''Dads can be a pain sometimes, but yours loves you, Heather. He's just having trouble finding balance.''

''How would you know?''

Darcie had to tread carefully here. She didn't want to lose the girl before she had a chance to form a bond. ''Because I've spent several weeks talking to you on the phone. You're a good girl, Heather, caring and sweet and smart. Those qualities come from being loved.''

''I guess. I miss my grandma, though.''

Darcie found it odd that Heather mentioned missing her grandmother rather than her mother. She knew Heather's mom had died five months ago.

Flynn had told her himself—after several shots of whiskey.

"When did your grandma leave?"

"About three weeks ago. Aunt Lois fell and broke her hip or something and Grandma had to stop taking care of us and go take care of her." She shrugged. "It feels weird in the house without her."

"Did she always live with you?"

"No. Just since Mary Beth was born."

And now Heather had to assume a larger share of the adult responsibilities in the O'Grady household at a time when she should be enjoying a carefree youth. Darcie understood that all family members— regardless of age—needed to pull together and do their part, but she still felt bad for Heather, for the obvious pain and hurting that would cause the girl to cry out for help by way of the runaway hot line.

They were quiet for a moment, and Darcie pulled back, sensing that Heather had shown enough of her vulnerabilities for the moment. And Darcie's own vulnerabilities were about to eat her alive. This was Flynn O'Grady's daughter, and she longed to just hold her, to fix her, to love her the way she loved Heather's father.

Impossible. Darcie knew that much better than most.

Feeling an ache born of hopelessness, she stood and looked around. "It's pretty cold out here."

"It's okay."

Good thing Darcie had a lot of patience. It could

get trying when a young person was determined to disagree—or to make a point not to totally agree—with everything an adult said.

"So what is it about this park that's special to you?"

Heather thought about not answering. Her feelings were private. And it was different talking to Darcie on the phone. It felt more anonymous. Face-to-face made those scary emotions do freaky things to her brain, made her feel stupid and embarrassed. But Darcie wasn't looking at her like she was stupid.

"This is where my mom used to take me when I was little." Heather watched as her breath puffed out in a white cloud. "She would push me on the swings and hold my hand when I went down the slide. And she laughed a whole lot back then." Oh, God, the hurt inside was really bad.

"You miss your mom."

"I guess." She hated admitting to a need. "I miss Grandma, too, but at least she's not dead."

"I'm sorry about your mother, sweetie. I don't know what it's like to lose a parent. As much as my mom and I fight, I can't imagine being without her."

Heather looked up. Most people said they knew what it felt like, even if they didn't. Darcie Moretti spoke honestly. And she didn't talk down to her or shy away from sad subjects. "Do you, like, live with your mom still?"

Darcie laughed. "No. I have my own place, but sometimes I wonder why I shell out the money. I'm at my folks' house a lot. Mealtimes especially. Ma takes it as a personal affront if I don't show up for pot roast."

Heather gave a wistful smile. "Grandma makes a pretty good pot roast."

"A lot of problems and worries seem smaller over a bowl of mashed potatoes and pot roast." Darcie heard the rumble of Heather's stomach. "I bet you got so upset with your dad, you forgot to eat."

Heather giggled, looking slightly embarrassed that her stomach had made such a loud noise.

"How would you feel about coming home with me? You'd be doing me a big favor," she added quickly when Heather looked as though she was going to object. "I got tied up earlier and missed dinner. This is one of the unforgivable sins in a household like mine. Especially on Wednesdays and Sundays. If you don't show, you'd better be dead or have a good reason why you're not there."

"But it's nearly nine o'clock."

"Doesn't matter. A missed meal is a major cause for drama and lectures, with a huge helping of guilt so you don't repeat the infraction. Ma's side of the family is Irish and German and Dad's is Italian. I imagine you can guess what sort of dramatics fly with a combination like that."

"Do they yell at you?"

"Heck, yes. They yell at me and the dog and the walls. It's an art families like ours learn at birth."

Heather giggled again.

"Honest," Darcie said, watching the softening, the acceptance, knowing she was on the verge of victory. She wanted that victory for Heather.

And she wanted it for Heather's father. Just the thought, the image of Flynn O'Grady nearly side-tracked her.

"Grandma talks to the wall, and Mom talks to thin air. 'She says she's coming, then doesn't show her mother the courtesy of a phone call. A body could be lying dead in the gutter, but does she bother to call her mother? No. And here I have a nice chicken in the pot going to waste,'" Darcie mimicked, waving her arms like a conductor for emphasis, pleased by the way Heather's face stretched farther into a grin. "You really don't want to leave me alone to face that, do you?"

Heather stood. "What did she cook tonight?"

Darcie stood, too, barely restraining the urge to reach out, to make sure Heather didn't walk off. "Roast chicken and stuffing. And chocolate cake."

"I guess I could come for dinner."

Darcie led Heather to the car, wondering if she would beat Flynn to Trenton, if she'd have a chance to form a bond with his daughter, to talk her into going home and staying there. She wondered if there would be enough time for the Moretti clan to work their magic as they had so many times in the past.

She prayed that there would be. She couldn't lose a kid to the streets. It hurt too much.

Now that she knew it was Flynn O'Grady's daughter at stake, it was all the more important to her. It was personal.

DARCIE DEBATED having a second piece of choco-late cake.

"Oh, go on," Grandma Connor urged. "Your thighs won't appreciate it, but life's short."

Rose Moretti raised her gaze to the ceiling as though seeking divine patience. Darcie decided that her mother had really perfected that look. "She insults her own granddaughter, right here in my kitchen. I ask you, is this the way to act?" Though Ma was German-born, thirty-five years of living with an Italian man had added to her repertoire of gestures and voice nuances.

"Of course it is. If family can't tell the truth, it's a sad day. Besides, she's growing a baby in her womb and every little girl has to learn about chocolate."

Darcie's hand jerked and her next forkful of cake landed icing down on the china plate. She wanted to put a muzzle on Grandma Connor, but knew from thirty-one years of experience that it wouldn't do any good. Grandma said what she wanted, when she wanted.

And that could well be a problem. Especially with Flynn coming over. She hadn't yet told her family the identity of her baby's father. And thankfully they hadn't pushed her. Now, all she needed was for Grandma to mention the baby before she had a chance to talk to Flynn.

Trying not to think about any more disasters, Darcie forked a bite of the sinful dessert into her mouth, noticing that Heather had stopped eating and was watching to see if anyone had actually taken offense over the fat comments. The way Rose and Grandma were nose to nose, it sure looked like war.

"Hopefully this baby won't inherit my tendencies to gain weight. And hopefully she'll have more will-power."

"You're not fat," Heather said cautiously.

"Of course she's not!" Rose agreed, shooting another glare at her mother, which Grandma ignored with a sniff. "And Grandma does not think so, either. She just likes to hear herself talk. Trouble is, she lets anything that comes into her brain just rip right from her lips."

"And you don't?" Grandma asked, making a face.

Darcie couldn't help it. She laughed. And so did Heather.

"I told you, didn't I?"

Heather nodded. Both Rose and Grandma hid smiles. They were putting on a show. That it appeared to be at Darcie's expense wasn't a problem. Darcie understood them, knew she was loved.

"So, tell me about this ogre of a father you have."

"Grandma!" Darcie said.

"Well, a girl runs away from home it must be that she is living with a beast."

"He's not really a beast," Heather said, her fork suspended half way to her mouth.

"No? What is he, then?"

"An architect."

"A businessman. Good sturdy stock. That's important. And you have brothers and sisters?"

"A little sister. She's one."

Grandma nodded, her twinkling gaze darting to

Darcie. "So he is a nice boy. A businessman, father, good husband material. My granddaughter should find such a man. A single one, that is."

"Grandma, stop." Darcie wondered if her guilt was flashing across her forehead. She'd already found Flynn O'Grady. And he *was* single.

Her face heated and she grew uncomfortably warm beneath her coat. Her mother was still frowning and shooting looks at Darcie over wearing her coat in the kitchen. But she'd rather sweat. She didn't want to give Flynn a heart attack when he showed up. He'd had enough upsets for one night.

Already she could feel herself chickening out of telling him. At least for tonight.

"What, a grandmother can't have a conversation?" Grandma Connor gave Darcie a long, probing look, then turned her attention back to Heather. "And how about your mama?"

Heather lowered her eyes, pushed her glass of milk back and forth on the maple table. "My mom died."

Rose was across the room in an instant, her pillow-soft arms wrapped around Heather, her snapping gaze shooting licks of flame at Grandma Connor.

"Ah, darling, such a tragedy. You must forgive us for prying."

Heather wanted to cry but was determined not to. Darcie's mom smelled of chocolate pudding and love. The kitchen was warm from the oven and stove, yet the furnace kicked on. The house was modest, a narrow duplex with a small front yard, where the kitchen was the hub of the family and the neighbors were a holler away.

Totally different from the house she and her dad and Mary Beth lived in outside of Princeton. The O'Grady house was large—a hoity-toity upper-class house Robbie Sanders had told her once. It sat on an acre of wooded land surrounded by apple and oak trees and pitch pines.

Heather decided that she'd trade fancy for homey any day. She liked these comforting arms around her. And truthfully, she was kind of tickled by Grandma Connor. She didn't want to spoil everything by acting all sad and upset.

"That's okay," she said to Rose. "I'm over it."

"Of course you're not. No one ever gets over losing a mother. But we'll talk of more happy topics, shall we?"

"Men are happy topics," Grandma muttered. "I especially like the ones with tattoos. Your daddy got any of those tattoos?"

Rose threw up her hands, Darcie choked on a swallow of cake and everyone jumped when there was a loud knock at the door.

"I'll get it," Darcie said, hopping up. Passing her mother, she whispered, "Put a cork in Grandma, would you?"

"You know she has a mind of her own," Rose said, not even bothering to lower her voice. "I'll see if your father can do anything with her. And when are you going to take off that moth-eaten coat?"

Darcie ignored her mother's last question, pulled open the door and felt her knees go weak at the sight of Flynn O'Grady. He wore a long black overcoat, dress shoes that probably didn't have a lot of traction against the icy stoop and a tie decorated with pictures of hot sauce bottles and chili peppers. Mary Beth was cradled in his arms, all bundled up in a furry pink snowsuit.

"Is she here?" he asked.

All conversation behind them stopped. She turned and looked at Heather, who went through several emotions at record speed. They flashed across her face like neon on an Atlantic City marquee—relief, elation, love, then suspicion, rebellion and accusation. This last was aimed at Darcie.

Darcie left Flynn to make his own way inside and went to Heather. The girl stood, backed up. "You told him?"

"Heather—"

"I trusted you. How come you called him?"

"I didn't call him. I was at Hardware and Muffins when the hot line paged me. That's where The Daddy Club meets."

"So you what, told him everything?"

"No," Darcie said softly. "Not everything. But you gave me your name, Heather, your full name, as well as your father's. If you wanted anonymity you wouldn't have done that." The girl was silent, casting furtive glances over Darcie's shoulder at Flynn. "Would you?" Darcie prompted.

Heather shrugged. "I guess." It was her standard noncommittal answer, the underlying meaning lurking beneath the tone.

Darcie heard the interpretation as though it were a shout.

"Give him a chance, sweetie. He's really upset."

Heather tried to keep the belligerent look on her face, but she couldn't. The minute her dad moved toward her, she lost it. A sob escaped and she slipped right into his arms, burrowing into his chest.

"You scared me half to death, sweetheart."

"I was scared, too, Daddy." She inhaled and hiccuped on a laugh. "You've got mushy crackers on your tie. That's gross."

Mary Beth squealed and boinked Heather on the head with drool-slick fingers. The kid should seem like a nuisance. But she wasn't. Not really. Heather hugged her dad some more, then took the baby from his arms, determined to show her off. This was one of those instances where a baby came in handy. She was a buffer. Plus nobody could resist a little kid. Heather liked the attention the baby brought, even if she sometimes had to take a back seat to her. She could always pretend that it was for her, too.

Proudly she turned and walked over to Grandma Connor. "This is Mary Beth," she introduced.

Grandma ran a wrinkled finger over Mary Beth's cheek, then turned her eyes onto Heather, reaching out to pat her hair. "You're a good girl. You do your family proud." Heather didn't really understand the praise, but she understood the look. It meant that she was special, and just as important as the baby was.

"We should be going, Heather," Flynn said.

Heather's stomach dipped. She wasn't ready to go yet. He didn't seem mad that she'd run away, but she was pretty sure he was gonna yell when they were alone. Well, he never really *yelled,* but it felt like it anyway. He'd probably just ground her again, though technically she was already grounded, so that wouldn't be any big deal.

Thankfully Darcie's mother saved the moment.

"Of course you should not be going! You haven't had dessert! Did you eat a meal? I could warm up a nice plate of chicken for you."

"No, really, I've eaten—"

"Then cake. You've not eaten chocolate cake, have you?"

"No—"

"Good. Sit. I'll get you a plate and milk."

Darcie was tickled by the look on Flynn's face as her mother steamrollered him. "Might as well sit," she said. "You'll never hear the end of it if you don't."

"Watch your tongue," Rose admonished.

Flynn glanced at Darcie just in time to see her lick her lips. His hand tightened on the back of the chair and his movements stilled for a split second.

To his everlasting horror, the two older ladies honed right in on his pause and the reason for it.

Flynn felt his ears burn, knew his face was beet red. Man, he hadn't even been formally introduced to these women, yet they knew that he was thinking erotic thoughts about Darcie's tongue. It was there in the twinkle of their eyes, in the way they practically tossed a cup of milk and his plate of cake in front of him and scooted Heather and Mary Beth out of the room on some pretense of showing them off to someone called Johnny.

Chapter Three

"I take it that was your mom and grandmother?" He sat down and tried to focus on the wedge of chocolate cake in front of him rather than on sexy thoughts of Darcie Moretti.

"Yes. Rose and Edna."

"And Johnny's your father?"

"Smart and good-looking, too," she quipped. "Want me to call them all back for introductions?"

"Let's give it a few. Let me quit blushing."

"You were thinking about watching my tongue?"

He nearly choked on a sip of milk. "You are direct."

"Is there any other way to be?"

"Well…yes." He felt off balance, *shy,* for crying out loud. His memories of Darcie were vivid and fresh in his mind. He took a bite of dessert, glad of the distraction. "Cake's good."

"Ma makes the best." She sat down across from him. "What's going through your mind?"

"Too many things to name." He put down his fork and took another sip of milk. There was something about this homey kitchen that made him feel welcome, made him reluctant to leave. But he didn't belong here. He needed to learn to handle his family life—his children—on his own. Enrolling in The Daddy Club was a step in the right direction, a desperate measure after being backed against the wall and not knowing where else to turn. He couldn't allow himself to idealize the Morettis or anyone else as fairy godmothers, ready to swoop in and smooth out the wrinkles of his home life. "I appreciate you finding Heather."

"She was at Hawkins Park."

Flynn pushed his empty plate away and gazed up at the ceiling. "I should have known that," he said, his voice both soft and rough. "It's where Marsha used to take her."

"Your wife."

"Yeah." Her tone surprised him, had a strained ring to it. But when he looked at her, nothing appeared amiss. Just as well. He didn't want to talk about Marsha now. Too many whammies had blindsided him today. His nerves were raw and a breath away from splintering.

"Heather's changed a lot in the past few months, and for the life of me, I can't figure out how to get through to her. I had no idea she would ever think of running away."

"You probably did, if you think back."

"Maybe. It's tough, though, you know? I'm dealing with a thirteen-year-old who doesn't speak my language and a one-year-old who doesn't speak *any* language!"

Darcie burst out laughing, the sound exuberant and refreshing, touching something deep in his battered soul. He didn't realize how much he needed spontaneous laughter in his life, how much he needed a friend.

"Guess I sounded a little dramatic, huh?"

"No. Typical father of a teenager."

"Thank God I'm typical." Feeling lighter, he tipped back the kitchen chair, balancing on the rear legs. "I thought I was a total alien!"

"You're a handsome alien."

There was that directness again. Slowly he lowered the chair legs back to the linoleum floor, his gaze holding hers. He noticed beads of perspiration on her face, then glanced at her wool coat. "Aren't you too warm in that jacket?"

She made a figure eight in a mound of spilled sugar on the maple table and didn't look at him. "I'm fine."

When he put his hand over hers, he felt her jolt of awareness. Darcie Moretti was attracted to him and doing her darnedest to act otherwise. He'd known it that night five months ago, and it was evident tonight. "What happened to you that night? Why did you leave?"

Because you called me Marsha. She shrugged. "I had to go. You were asleep so I left you that way."

She wasn't ready for this turn of conversation, didn't have her words planned out. She liked to be in control, liked to know where every period and comma belonged, liked to *fix* things. All on her terms though. She didn't care to be caught off guard like this.

He ran his thumb over the freckles on the back of her hand. "I looked for you in Philly. You led me to believe you lived there."

This time she didn't evade. "Maybe I did. It felt easier somehow. I don't normally go to bed with guys I've just met." *Just ones I've been in love with all my life.* "I was saving us both the embarrassment of the morning after."

"We didn't just meet, Darcie. I've known you since you were a kid."

"Known *of* me, maybe, but you didn't really know me." The timing had always been off for them. When she was thirteen, he'd been the older boy who made her breath catch and her dreams sweet, but he hadn't even known she was alive. He'd been wrapped up in football and cheerleaders, making her young heart weep with jealousy. Then at eighteen, she'd been the wrong social class and her fantasies had suffered a stinging death when the society page had gone gaga over his country club wedding to Marsha Levine, the district attorney's daughter.

At thirty-one, Darcie's fantasies had been resurrected when she'd encountered him in a hotel bar, both of them single, alone and all grown up. And she had seen her chance to put her fantasies to rest, operating on the theory that experiencing him would end her obsession.

Boy, had that been convoluted reasoning.

"I'd like the chance to get to know you now," Flynn said, jolting her out of her musing.

His fingers stroked across hers lightly, making it hard to concentrate. And she was sure there was a reason she needed to remember all her faculties, to keep up her guard. But the firm shape of his lips was distracting, the smooth, deep tone of his voice mesmerizing.

She pulled her hand from beneath his, sat back in her chair, took a long breath.

A dimple creased his cheek. "Did that make you nervous?"

"Maybe." She crossed her arms, then realized how that molded her coat to her body, and quickly uncrossed them.

"I'm very curious about you, Darcie Moretti, and intrigued…. I'm attracted to you and telling myself it's not wise to pursue."

Darcie licked her suddenly dry lips. They had a maple table between them. The smell of chocolate cake permeated the air. The heat of the furnace fogged the kitchen window that was edged with ice. All very homey and comfy and perfectly innocent, and yet she had the most overpowering urge to jump his bones. Oh, this was unacceptable.

And because it was unacceptable, she laughed. She didn't know what else to do. She did know that she ought to head him off at the pass.

"For heaven's sake, don't just *tell* yourself not to pursue me—shout it."

His brown-eyed gaze locked on to her, pinning her in the chair, making her heart speed up. Then his lips curved and before he even spoke, she knew she was a goner.

"So," he began in that deep, sexy voice, "it seems you're just as intrigued. Which means, I'm thinking…that you wouldn't stop me if I, say…kissed you?"

The cuff of his dress shirt rode up on his wrist, revealing a silver watch. His hands were bold and strong—the kind of hands that were experienced in giving a woman pleasure. She knew that only too well.

She scooted back her chair. "We're in my mother's kitchen."

"I didn't mean right this minute."

He was giving her a fair warning—a sensual warning. And it was thrilling.

And scary as all get-out.

There was still one big hurdle she needed to cross with him. But, oh the chemistry between them was like a dancing flame—hot and seductive, mesmerizing. She shook her head, wishing she dared take off her coat.

His sexy smile creased dimples beside his mouth, crinkling the corners of his eyes. "I can't believe I've made you speechless. Darcie the bold."

"Darcie the sensible. Can you imagine my mother or grandmother walking in here, catching us looking at each other like animals in heat?" *Oh, good grief.* She held up a hand. "Forget I said that. Just give me a minute to find a hole to sink into."

He laughed. "I like you, Darcie Moretti."

Her traitorous heart gave a glad leap. She more

than *liked* Flynn O'Grady. "Shh, Ma and Grandma will be in here to see what they're missing out on. And then we'd all be in big trouble, because they're forever trying to fix me up with somebody—male, that is." Well, there she went again, putting her foot in it. She needed some glue for her lips.

"I'm all for being fixed up."

"*You* can make light of it, but then you get to go home and never hear from them again. I have to put up with their nagging." She pushed at her hair, adjusted a chopstick that was slipping. "They live to give me flak."

"Does that bother you?"

"It would bother me if they *didn't* nag."

He nodded, his chocolate eyes letting her know she might be off the hook for now, but that he was reserving the right to pick up the sensual thread at a moment's notice.

It was a terribly unsettling look.

"I wish Heather would adopt that attitude."

"What?" She was having trouble keeping up. "Oh, you mean about nagging? She's not as against you as you might think, Flynn. But she's dealing with a lot lately."

His brow rose.

She held up her hands in defense, remembering his pique in the rest room when she'd stated a similar conclusion. "I'm not outlining your perceived failures, or assuming to know all about your circumstances."

"Yes, you are," he said softly.

That caught her off guard, and for a minute she

went silent. Then she laughed softly. "Okay, so I am. Sorry. Sue me. It's a curse."

"A good curse. You care."

"Yes, I do. A great deal. And I want what's best for Heather."

"Then give me some pointers."

"Be patient with her. Try to remember what it was like when you were her age."

"Man alive, what do you think I've *been* doing? That's exactly why I'm so concerned about her!"

"Shame on you, O'Grady. I wasn't talking about sex."

"Yeah? Well, every young boy is thinking it when he looks at Heather."

"You mean Robbie Sanders?"

"For one. He's in high school. He's got no business sniffing around a thirteen-year-old."

Darcie bit her lips to keep from laughing. He was so endearingly old-fashioned.

"What?" he demanded.

She shook her head and laughed. "Nothing. You're just so predictable. A typical father who's resisting his little girl growing up into a woman."

"Don't even say that." He shuddered, and Darcie laughed even harder.

"You need to trust her, Flynn. She's got a good head on her shoulders. She's just going through adolescent changes, and she's confused. But I believe she'll make the right decision in the end."

"She's only thirteen. She's too young to make decisions—"

She pressed a finger to his lips, raised a brow.

A sensual fire ignited like an inferno in Flynn's gut. He reached up, cupped her hand and held it in place. Just to see what she would do, he kissed her finger. She drew in a shaky breath.

Their eyes held over their clasped hands. And by damn, he liked that interest he saw in hers, the swift desire.

Flynn wasn't sure how or when it had happened, but he'd lost any thread of their conversation. His gaze kept straying to her mouth. Those full lips. The freckles surrounding them, fanning out to her cheeks, her nose, her forehead, the golden flecks dusting the backs of her hands, expressive hands that gestured with wild abandon, yet with grace.

A burst of canned laughter sounded from the television in the living room. Mary Beth's delighted squeal mingled with conversation and a sitcom rerun.

Flynn raised his eyes back to hers.

Her indrawn breath was swift and telling. "What *is* it with us?" she asked.

He didn't need clarification of her question. The chemistry between them was palpable. Just like it had been that night at the hotel. "It's pretty strong."

She stood, fanned herself. "This is a really bad idea, but let's go outside."

He didn't have to be asked twice. His daughters were well chaperoned and happy. Darcie had said that her family had a knack for soothing the ruffled feathers of hormonal teens. He would continue to give them time to work their magic. And he would take some time for himself, some sorely needed time for himself. Time with a pretty woman on the front porch. A woman he'd been dreaming of for the past five months.

Darcie held the door for Flynn and closed it behind them, inhaling the crisp night air, allowing it to cool her body and her runaway hormones.

Pines and leafy bushes that had survived winter's frost surrounded the porch. Concrete steps led down to a postage-stamp-size yard that was sliced in two sections by a walkway—a cookie-cutter version of every other yard on the block. Across the street, the neighbors still had their Christmas lights up, though the twinkling strands sagged where wind and snowfall had pulled out the staples.

The snow had stopped but the smell of rain was in the air. Cold bit at her cheeks, but her insides were burning.

She turned and gazed at Flynn's tie. It wasn't like her to feel shy, but she suddenly did. "You're awfully dressed up."

"I had a meeting with a new client."

"Not at a job site, I take it?"

"Sort of. It's a house over in New Brunswick. A remodel of a Victorian built in the early 1900s."

His breath ballooned in front of him, warming her cheeks. "I thought Ula Mae said you did commercial architecture." Ula Mae seemed to know everyone and everything going on in the state of New Jersey. And she was more than happy to pass it along. Since Darcie saw a lot of the older woman—mostly when they were discussing investments or insurance over an espresso at Hardware and Muffins—she usually got an earful of tidbits about the people in the community.

"I do both," Flynn said, his dimples flashing a sexy warning. "What else does Ula Mae say about me?"

For the life of her, Darcie couldn't come up with a witty quip. His utter charm and good looks snagged her, held her. "Uh, plenty."

His grin widened. "Shall we see if I measure up?"

"That's not..." *Necessary,* she finished silently.

Slowly, purposefully, he pulled her to him. Her heart slammed against her chest as he molded her body to his.

She knew exactly how this man measured up.

Desire raged like a flash point fire. Her belly wasn't yet so big that she couldn't feel his erection against the vee of her thighs.

"What have you got under that coat?"

His question brought reality crashing around her, nearly making her faint. She stared at his lips, then his eyes. Why couldn't he have just kissed her and asked questions later?

Time had just run out.

"Uh, there's something I've been meaning to tell you."

His lips touched hers, and she groaned. The fire between them was still as strong as ever. And *she* needed to be strong. She eased back.

"I'm...uh, pregnant."

For what seemed like endless moments, he simply stared at her, his expression utterly blank. Then his forehead pleated and his body went rigid as he visibly struggled to process what she had said. "You're...?"

"I'm going to have your baby."

Chapter Four

Flynn leaped back, stunned, needing to sit before he fell. "You're having my…" My God, he couldn't even finish the sentence. He'd need those Daddy Club meetings more than ever now, he thought stupidly.

"I didn't mean to catch you off guard."

He didn't know whether to laugh or strangle her. He stared at the front of her coat, realizing now why she'd kept the baggy thing on.

A baby? His? What had he been thinking that night? He was a man who cherished family, had always wanted a big one—despite the ineptness he was currently displaying with the one he had—but he was normally more careful with a woman. Protected her.

"Let me see."

Darcie suddenly felt embarrassed. With trembling fingers, she slipped the buttons through their loops, spread the panels, felt her heart gallop out of control as he eased away from the porch wall and came toward her, never taking his eyes off her belly.

At only five months along, she wasn't hugely pregnant, but there was a definite swell beneath her charcoal jersey-knit tunic.

He reached out as though to touch, then pulled back. "Are you sure—"

Her chin jutted out and she didn't let him finish his sentence. She didn't need to. "Am I sure it's yours?" Offended, hurt, she clenched her teeth. That damned class distinction that had made her feel like a waif at thirteen and again at eighteen rose up to haunt her. She thought she'd outgrown the insecurity. She hadn't.

She stepped back, took a breath, told herself she would *not* cry. "You know, why don't we just forget this whole thing, okay? We'll just deal with getting Heather to go home with you and that will be that."

"Darcie..." He reached for her.

She slapped his hand away. "I might have given you the wrong impression that night in Philly when I hopped right into bed with you, but I'm *not* like that. I'm not loose."

"Ah, damn it." This time he evaded her swatting hands, and cupped her face. "I know you're not."

"How? You don't know me."

"Instincts, then." His thumbs massaged her temples.

She sniffed, mortified that the tears had slipped down her cheeks despite her strict efforts to hold them back. He should be hurling questions at her, yet instead he gave her tenderness.

"Your instincts are awful," she said, not even

knowing why she said it. Nothing made sense right now.

He eased her close. "Why in the world didn't you tell me sooner?"

Her breath caught on a suppressed sob and she shrugged. Admitting that she was a chicken didn't seem adequate for the moment.

He didn't push. He simply held her closer. "It'll be okay."

"No it won't."

"Shh." His palms were cold against her cheeks, his fingers gentle where they outlined the shell of her ear, cupped the back of her head. His head lowered, paused.

With exquisite care, he removed the colorful barrettes and chopsticks from her hair. Masses of naturally curly hair tumbled down, tangling with his fingers. Pinpricks raised goose bumps on her scalp and her arms. The roots of her hair hurt from being held up for so many hours, but his steady massage soothed…and inflamed.

Unconsciously she pressed against him. His gaze moved to hers, so strong and sure and utterly focused, holding her like a soft caress. She shivered, heard a silent click in her brain and knew she was already in too deep, knew too that there was nothing she could do to turn off her traitorous emotions.

The sound of her moan was lost in his mouth as his lips finally closed over hers. The jolt was almost too much to stand. She jumped, pulled back for an instant and once more met the heat of his eyes.

"Easy," he whispered.

He took her lips again and heard her say, "Trouble."

Yes. Definitely trouble. But it was the sweetest kind. The explosion of emotions that burst through him took him by surprise. Darcie Moretti was no shrinking violet when it came to giving and taking…or kissing. She didn't play games or wait for him to lead. She participated, gave it her all. And man alive! What that "all" did to him.

He'd had his thirty-sixth birthday, and lately he'd been feeling jaded and old. With the simple, avid press of Darcie's lips, he suddenly felt young and renewed.

He angled her head for better access and dove into the kiss, forgetting that Darcie's family and his own daughters were on the other side of the door. He was caught up in some really glorious sensations, and for a while he just wanted to feel. Just that.

And he was feeling a *lot*—the soft warmth of her mouth, the pillowy feeling of her plump lips pressed to his, the heat of her thighs where they made a perfect cradle for his erection. Her pregnant belly was firm and spooned right into his stomach as though their bodies were made to fit that way….

As though the Almighty had made each with the other in mind.

And that thought scared him, big-time.

Darcie could hardly breathe, and then decided that breathing was overrated. There was a certain thrill in the dizziness born of lack of oxygen. At that moment, she was certain that she could sustain her life on Flynn's taste alone—chocolate cake and milk and masculinity…and yes, trouble.

His kiss was sure and strong, yet soft and seductive. The joy he created with just that touch was potent, liberating. She wanted to go on forever, to take it further, to press closer, skin to skin.…

The porch light winked on and off. Darcie's eyes popped open and she leaped back from Flynn, her breath heaving, puffing white in the cold night air.

"Grandma Connor," she explained, struggling for breath. "She used to do that to me when I was a teenager, too. It meant my dad was out of his chair and I was in danger of being caught."

Flynn gave a strained laugh. "Been a while since I've worried about being caught necking on a girl's front porch."

"Yeah. Me, too. And that was pretty incredible."

His dimples flashed, illuminated by the yellow porch light. "I could fall for you real easy, Darcie Moretti. I know that sounds weird with you being pregnant and all."

Steady, she cautioned herself. *Don't jump.* "Good thing we're both sensible adults. And good thing neither of us has time to devote to a relationship."

He took a step closer. She took a step back. "Who says I don't have time for a relationship?" Never mind that she was right. It bothered him that she was thinking for him again.

"Your daughter does. Every time she calls the hot line. She's your number one concern, Flynn. And mine. I won't lose another kid."

"Another one?" Flynn asked. It was difficult to

think straight with desire still raging through him like a wildfire. But Darcie's tone flashed warning signals in his sluggish brain, making him uneasy. Even more upsetting was her including his daughter in that category of kids whom someone could lose. "Are you talking 'lose' as in dead?"

She looked away. "It happens sometimes."

He touched her cheek, turned her face back to him. "What happened to you?" he asked softly. "Who did you lose?"

"My best friend in high school."

Not so recent, he realized, relaxing now that he was fairly sure she wasn't talking about her hot line and his daughter. "Want to talk about it?"

"Are you sure you're ready to hear this?"

"Yes." No. He had an idea that as a father her story would cause him nightmares. But he wanted to know what made Darcie Moretti tick. And this was something that affected her deeply.

"Tammy's dad was pretty strict, more so than most, and he wasn't one to budge when he felt strongly about something. He'd been raising Tammy by himself, then one day he went to Atlantic City and came back married. Turns out he'd been seeing the woman for a while, but he'd never said a word to anybody, not even Tammy. He just brought Glenda home and expected Tammy to accept her new stepmother."

"And she didn't?"

"No. From then on, she went out of her way to be a rebel. She was bullheaded—a lot like your Heather, but older. She got pregnant and panicked."

Flynn flinched and Darcie realized she probably shouldn't have mentioned Heather and "pregnant" in the same breath.

"All Tammy thought about was that her dad was going to kill her. So instead of facing him, she ran away."

Darcie leaned a hip on the brick half wall that surrounded the porch, and plucked a couple of berries off a juniper bush. "I was the last person she called. I didn't think she was serious about staying gone. She'd threatened so many times before. I told her I'd come meet her, and she got mad at me and said I'd probably just tell my mom and then my mom would call her stepmom." She glanced back at Flynn. "You know how it is with parents or neighbors sticking together."

Cold bit at her cheeks and her insides as though an arctic blizzard had suddenly swept the yard. She could still see Tammy's laughing face, still vividly remember the horror and then the giggles when they'd wrestled over a swing in grade school and Darcie had ended up with a broken finger.

Wanting to cry, determined not to, she tossed the berries over the side of the porch into the dirty slush lining the walkway and straightened, feeling the welcome warmth emanating from Flynn's body as he moved closer.

"So what happened to Tammy?"

"After her phone call to me, nobody ever—" Her voice broke. "Nobody ever heard from her again."

He pulled her to him and held her close.

"I kept thinking that if I'd said something different that night, maybe she would have come home. Or if I'd just gone to meet her. That's why I always react to a kid who calls on the hot line. Even if they're just crying wolf, I still go. You never know. I don't want to blow it again.''

''You didn't blow it, Darcie.''

''Maybe not, but I still feel the guilt. And the pain.'' She could still remember the day the police had found Tammy's body. But she couldn't bring herself to go further into those horrible details with Flynn. Tammy had gotten into the car with the wrong person and ended up dead. And to this day her murderer had never been caught.

If Darcie truly let herself dwell on that last fact, her need for atonement would bury her.

She drew back, glanced at the front room picture window where lamplight filtered through the lace curtains. The television flickered green and blue, flashing illumination across the brick porch walls.

Flynn's daughter was safe inside those walls.

And Darcie would do everything in her power to make sure his daughter *stayed* safe.

She looked up at him, her full lips swollen from his kisses, her hazel eyes serious. ''Heather reminds me a lot of Tammy.''

Flynn drew in a swift breath. Panic and terror nearly doubled him over. ''But she can talk to me! I'm not that strict.''

''I didn't say she was exactly like her, Flynn.'' She put a gentle hand on his arm, to soothe, but also to telegraph the importance of her words. ''But she's mixed up. She's having trouble adjusting to the changes in her body, in her life. Just like you are. If she calls me again, I want to be there for her. If I let her down, who's she going to turn to?''

"Me."

"What if she won't? I'm not trying to scare you. Well, maybe I am a little. But Heather has to be our first concern. That's one of the reasons why we can't repeat that kiss, why we have to stay neutral.''

"Darcie, for crying out loud, you're having my baby!'' He raked a hand through his hair and glared at her as though the force of his look alone should make her back down.

It didn't.

He hissed out a sigh, relaxed his macho stance. "What if Heather gave us her seal of approval?''

"She hasn't, so that's not an issue right now. Besides I've got a lot to do before my baby's born—''

"*Our* baby.''

"I don't have the time or the energy to have an affair.''

"I didn't say—''

"What?'' she interrupted. "You had commitment and marriage in mind?''

He looked shell-shocked, like she'd hit him over the head with a brick. And though she'd successfully made her point, his reaction hurt.

"Good thing I'm not in the market for marriage either,'' she said, trying for flippant, knowing by the crack in her voice that she'd failed.

"I didn't say I wouldn't marry you. You just caught me off guard.''

The conversation was deteriorating. "I didn't ask

for marriage, Flynn. Haven't you been listening? Marriage is the furthest thing from my mind. And it's totally out of the question for us.''

"Why?"

"Because of Heather!" She was so distraught, she couldn't keep the frustration from her voice.

He slipped his arms around her and drew her against his chest. "We'll figure something out, Darc."

"It's not just between us anymore, Flynn. And I won't sacrifice one child for another."

The porch light clicked on and stayed on this time. Darcie believed her argument. And for tonight he'd have to let it be. He had to get Heather home, make her understand how much he loved her, how hard he was trying.

He was like a drowning man. But he had to think, be aware, make sure Heather knew she was loved. By him.

The knowledge that she'd considered running away terrified him. They were a family. And he was determined to do better. Be better.

And then there was Darcie and the baby. Man, this was a lot for one man to handle in a day.

He sighed. "We need to talk about this, Darcie. Make some plans.''

She shook her head.

"I know. Not now." He glanced up as the curtains twitched. "But this isn't finished."

STILL SHAKEN over last night's events, Flynn drove Heather to school the next morning, unable to face her riding the bus. He didn't want to take away her freedom, but he wasn't ready just yet to give her a lot of rein.

And now he was in the parking lot of Darcie's apartment building, a four-story brick structure with a fire escape climbing the back wall.

She'd refused to discuss the pregnancy with him last night. But he'd meant what he'd said. They *would* talk. Now that he'd gotten Heather settled— he hoped—and cleared his thinking a bit, they needed to plan.

He'd been abandoned by his father—granted, Flynn had been eighteen, but the sense of loss was still there. And his wife had abandoned him. It hurt to be left as though you were insignificant. He wouldn't let a child of his suffer those emotions.

Family was important—planned for or not.

Telling himself he was more calm this morning, he got Mary Beth out of her car seat, hitched the diaper bag over his shoulder and made his way up the stairs to the third-story hallway. It had been ridiculously easy to find her address in the book. Why hadn't he at least thought to look before? Because he'd truly believed she didn't live in the state of New Jersey. And he'd had his hands full with the kids.

But he'd thought of her. Often. Kept her memory tucked in a corner of his mind, a memory that he'd taken out and played again and again when the loneliness crept in, when the stress threatened to bow him.

He located 3A, knocked on the door and waited.

She'd told him she often worked from home and rarely went into the office before ten.

There was a peephole in the door. Was she on the other side looking at him? Avoiding him? She definitely hadn't wanted to have this conversation with him last night. For that matter, it had taken her a hell of a long time to tell him in the first place. And only then when he'd bumped right into the evidence.

He pounded harder on the door. Mary Beth thought this was a fine game and clapped his cheeks between her drool-slick hands, giving a giggle that started in her belly and erupted like sunshine.

He grinned and pounded on the door again. "Open up, Darcie."

"She ain't home."

Flynn whirled around. The neighbor across the hall in 3B stood in the doorway wearing a ratty bathrobe and an annoyed expression. "How do you know she's not home?"

"You're awful full of questions for a stranger pounding on a lady's apartment door. I'm calling a cop."

"No, wait. I'm a friend of Darcie's. Flynn O'Grady." He stepped across the hall and held out his hand.

"Bentley," the man responded, and reluctantly accepted the handshake.

Flynn indicated Mary Beth with a nod of his head. "I'm harmless, really. How often do you see burglars carrying a baby and a diaper bag?"

"Well, you got me there. But she's still not home. Gone for the week on insurance business. Girl works too hard, if you ask me. She's a whiz with investments. Got a knack for it and an uncanny sense for companies that are getting ready to take off. It's what she should be doing, I keep telling her.''

Flynn nodded, learning another tidbit about Darcie Moretti. Still, he didn't like the fact that she'd taken herself and their baby out of town without telling him. He had a responsibility here.

And she was making it damned hard for him to own up to it.

HEATHER STOOD in the middle of the living room listening to the snuffling noises Mary Beth made when she was waking up. Her dad had gone to town to copy some stupid blueprints. And she was stuck at home. For the past week, he'd been more out of it than usual.

At least she'd talked him out of calling Mrs. Wolinsky to baby-sit. Heck, she was thirteen. She could baby-sit herself *and* Mary Beth—even though that was a pain.

Well, not really. The baby was good. She was little and didn't have the memories of Mom like Heather did.

In a way that made Heather's heart soften with love, Mary Beth opened her eyes and blinked like a baby owl. Seeing Heather, she popped right up, gave a happy shriek and tossed a slobbery Beanie Babies toy over the side of her playpen, looking at Heather like she expected her to play or something. How could the kid go from sleep to awake so fast?

Heather hissed out a breath and snatched up her

sister. When Mary Beth giggled, Heather felt the dimple in her left cheek crease even though she made a stern effort not to crack a smile. This wasn't the time for playing and making googly eyes. She was mad—although she wasn't really sure why. The emotions churning inside her lately scared her.

"You're cute and all, but you're not really my job. You slobber and you're gross." She reached for the even grosser bean bag toy, gave it to her sister, then whirled around when she heard a noise behind her.

Flynn came to a halt in the foyer a few steps away from the living room. Heather's softly spoken, prickly words made his gut twist, made the inadequate feelings sneak past his guard.

Did she think it was that bad here? Without his mom here to pick up the slack, it was tough, sure. His brain was on overload, and he was sinking fast. Couldn't Heather see that he had plenty on his plate, that he was hanging on by a string, that he could use some help, that he was trying his best?

God knows he didn't mean to be preoccupied but he was on a killer deadline with this latest set of blueprints—thanks to an engineer who'd taken off to Costa Rica right in the middle of the job.

And then there was Darcie who'd told him she was pregnant in one breath and had dumped him in the next—and *then* gone out of town on business, preventing him from even trying to press the issue.

It all made him crazy.

Shouldn't Heather see that he was overwhelmed and want to help? Out of love, if nothing else?

Apparently not. She stood beneath the arched doorway with Mary Beth hitched on her hip and a mutinous expression on her young face.

Flynn prepared himself for teenage war—even though he wasn't sure which battle they were fighting and why.

"Heather, it hurts me when you're so upset all the time. I'm trying not to impose on you with babysitting, but we're a family. With Grandma gone, we've got to depend on one another, pitch in with jobs—"

Right before his tired eyes, she clouded up, her chin trembling, tears overflowing and spilling over her powdered and blushed cheeks. How in the world did she do that so fast?

And why did it make him feel so damned deficient and terrified?

She thrust the baby at him. "Grandma didn't make her my job!" *Her* meaning Mary Beth.

He grabbed the baby. Mary Beth responded to the tension and wailed.

Heather whirled and stomped away. A few seconds later, the bedroom door slammed.

He and Mary Beth both jumped.

Mary Beth cried louder.

Flynn began to sweat. And to swear silently. He felt like making it a family affair and sitting down in the middle of the floor and crying right along with his daughters.

"Need help?"

Flynn whirled toward the front door that was still

standing open, the wind blowing leaves into the foyer. He hadn't even noticed the cold.

Darcie all bundled up in a heavy wool coat with a scarf wrapped around her neck and gloves on her hands, stood on his porch, her dark blond brows raised, her sexy freckles playing peek-a-boo through her cold-reddened complexion.

He wanted to be annoyed by both her question and her perky demeanor. Of course he needed help. But he'd be damned if he'd ask for it with Heather's exit line accusation still stinging in his ears and twisting in his gut. And besides, he was still a little ticked at Darcie for not returning his phone calls, never mind the fact that she'd been out of town for a week. That, too, hadn't set well with him.

"God forbid somebody else should think I'm assigning a job," he said.

Darcie grinned, ignoring his sour disposition and invited herself in. Nice house, she thought, pulling off her gloves. Huge. A bit intimidating for a girl like her.

"Learning anything at The Daddy Club?" She plucked the baby out of his arms and laughed when he glared at her.

"I've only been to one session. And that one was cut short, remember?"

"I remember. Lucky for you that I stopped by, hmm?" She nuzzled Mary Beth's cheek and offered a pacifier decorated with pink bunnies that was clipped to the front of the baby's corded overalls. "There there, sweet girl. You're okay now. Sissy and Daddy don't mean to be so loud. Do they?"

Mary Beth appeared charmed that someone was at last talking to her. She thrust her slobbery Beanie Babies toy in Darcie's face. Darcie made an appropriately pleased noise and glanced over at Flynn.

Poor guy, he looked so endearingly confused. And so sexy, it wasn't fair. She had to remind herself why she was here. For Heather...who'd made *another* call to the hot line.

It was tough, though. She wanted to be here for herself. For *her* baby. Her and Flynn's baby.

"How do you do that?" he asked.

"Do what?"

"Stay so calm."

"It's easy. These girls aren't my twenty-four-hour-a-day responsibility. I'll expect you to return the favor when I'm pacing the floor with mine—" The words were out before she could call them back. Halfway through, her brain had said, "Quit, don't go there." But it was too late.

She ducked her head, pressed her lips to Mary Beth's cheek, then gave a nervous laugh and dodged the slobbery fingers determined to poke in her mouth.

Flynn stepped close, caught his daughter's hand and said softly, "I *do* intend to be there for you, Darcie."

Chapter Five

Darcie closed her eyes. "Let's not talk about that now."

"No? I came by your apartment looking for you. I'd never have pegged you as a coward, Darc."

"I had business."

"And my baby. We need to discuss that."

"Not now, okay?" She glanced up the stairs where Heather had disappeared.

"So if you don't want to talk, how come you're here?"

"I came to invite you to dinner at my folks' house." Actually, Mr. Bentley had told her about Flynn's visit and she knew she needed to face the music. Face him.

And before she'd known it, like a silly high school girl driving by her boyfriend's house to see if his car was in the drive, she'd found herself cruising by Flynn's place. After the second time around the block, she'd told herself she was an adult and that as such, she could handle herself just fine.

So she'd stopped...and walked right into his chaos.

The timing wasn't good to talk about the two of them—the three of them, she amended, feeling the baby flutter inside her.

"You could have phoned," he pointed out.

She shrugged. She wasn't going to tell him of her foolishness of cruising his neighborhood. "It's Wednesday night—practically sacred in the Moretti household. Barring the plague or other natural disasters, they expect me to be at the table." He was making her nervous with the way he was looking at her. "So, do you want to come or not?"

"What about the girls?"

"Of course, the girls, too. Mom always has extras in case company drops by." A quick phone call and three extra places would be set at the supper table.

The problem was, could she hide her feelings from her family? It wouldn't take much for them to put two and two together and figure out that Flynn O'Grady was the father of her baby. All they'd have to do was look at the stars in Darcie's eyes.

"In that case, we'd love to come to dinner."

"You would?" Now she wasn't sure it was such a good idea. He was looking way too sexy for her peace of mind, although he was dressed simply in a gray T-shirt, a zip front sweatshirt, dark jeans and black sneakers. A big change from the business clothes of last week, but just as potent on her senses.

"It's noisy there. Grandma's been on Daddy all day about the cable interference. The service was interrupted during *Oprah* and she wanted Daddy to go straight to the cable office with his gun drawn.''

Flynn grinned and stepped closer, reaching out to catch Mary Beth's hand where it was trying to tie knots in Darcie's hair. Darcie's incredibly wild, incredibly soft hair... ''Your father often draws a gun on people?''

''Not anymore. He's retired from the Trenton PD. Grandma thinks that still carries weight.''

''I'm sure it does.'' She was nervous, he realized. And that intrigued him. ''Do you want to take back the invitation?''

She sighed, shook her head.

''Do they know about the baby?''

''Yes.''

''That I'm the father?''

''No.''

''Why?''

She glanced toward the stairs. ''I wasn't ready to tell anybody yet—at least not before I'd told you. Now, back to dinner... Whatever you do, don't side with Grandma. Daddy's disgusted with the whole argument. Don't let them suck you in.''

He saw her nervousness, wondered about her evasions, but allowed the subject change. She was right to be cautious. Mary Beth was too young to understand their conversation, but Heather wasn't. He wouldn't want her to wander downstairs and overhear. But they *would* discuss this subject. ''Better to have Grandma mad at me than Dad?''

''Yeah. He's quieter, but meaner.'' She grinned. ''And he'll call my brother and have him run your plates and be on the lookout for you next time you're over in Trenton. You'll be getting tickets for no good reason.''

''Your family's dangerous.''

''Not really. Just passionate—'' Uh-oh. Bad choice of words. She knew it by the way Flynn's eyes flared. ''I wasn't talking sex,'' she amended quickly.

''We could,'' he said, his dimple winking at her.

Her lips twitched. ''You're bad.''

''You started it.''

''Change the subject, Flynn.''

''I kind of like this one.'' At her narrowed look he held up his hands in a backing-off gesture. ''Okay, consider it changed. Give me a minute to go talk to Heather. For the life of me, I don't know what I keep doing wrong with her, but her tears and sadness is ripping my heart out.''

She gave him a look filled with compassion and passed Mary Beth back into his arms, her face flushing when his fingers brushed her breast. It couldn't be helped. With a wiggly one-year-old, you grabbed where you could to get a good hold and later apologized for any unintended intimacies. No big deal. So why was it suddenly difficult to draw a breath?

''Why don't I go talk to her? Actually, there's a class on fuses and circuit breakers at Hardware and Muffins tonight, the same time as The Daddy Club meets. Ordinarily a thirteen-year-old would be bored to death at something like that, but the ladies in Ruth Naomi's group are a crack-up. I think Heather will actually have fun. We can kill two birds, so to speak.

You get to do your thing and Heather can interact with the ladies and learn something to boot. Plus, Mary Beth will be properly fawned over—provided we make it out of my mom's house with her. Mom and Grandma are going to want to baby-sit. And you should say no, by the way," she told him, taking a breath, knowing she was running off at the mouth. But she was nervous.

"Why?"

Because my family and I don't need to fall any harder for you and your girls. Because I don't know if you're looking at me this way just because I'm having your baby. Because I can't be sure if it's me you're responding to or if I've trapped you.

"Because it'll be out of your way to go back and get the baby, and it's a school night for Heather."

"Then why should I be taking her out anyway?"

"We're not talking about a wild party, here, Flynn. You've got to give a little."

"Until it hurts, you mean?"

She patted him on the cheek. "It's gonna hurt for a whole lot of years to come. Get used to it."

"I don't think I'm going to survive."

"You'll survive. Ross Steadwell's Daddy Club will see to it."

"And you, Darcie Moretti? Will you see to it, too?"

God help her, when he used that deep, sexy tone of voice, she wanted to melt, to give in, to forget everything that was at stake.... Like a troubled teenager who could easily take the wrong path.

"I'm only inviting you to fried chicken and green beans. You're on you own with the lessons."

"Chicken," he said softly, and she knew he didn't mean the kind that was on their dinner menu.

"Darn right I am. I've made too many mistakes in my life. I'm not making another."

She saw him stiffen, saw a vein pulse at his temple. "I'm not sure I like you referring to my baby as a mistake."

This was getting too intimate. Too personal...too painful. "Now you're all of a sudden convinced it's your baby?"

"I don't deserve that, Darcie." His brows shifted into a frown. "I was shocked, yes, but I never doubted your word. If you hadn't hightailed it out of town you'd realize that."

"I'm sorry. And I don't consider her a mistake."

"Her?"

"Yes. And we really shouldn't be talking about this now." She glanced again at the stairs. "Which way to Heather's room?"

"Upstairs, third door on the right. The one with Snoopy Dog rap music blaring past the door."

Darcie laughed, releasing some of her tension. "Snoop Doggy Dogg, you mean."

"Whatever. It's one of those animals."

"Snoop Doggy is a fine artist." Though not always appropriate for a thirteen-year-old, she thought as she turned and headed up the stairs.

Flynn was right. The music was blaring. And Darcie had an idea that it was a deliberate attempt to be noticed rather than a desire to listen to those decibels. The minute she knocked on the door, the volume turned down.

"Go away!"

"Heather? It's me, Darcie. Can I come in?"

A pause. The music volume went down even lower. Then the door opened.

"How come you're here?" Heather wiped her dripping nose on her sleeve and gave Darcie a wary look.

"It's kind of dumb. I was driving by and the next thing I knew I was standing at your front door."

Heather rolled her eyes.

Darcie grinned. "I told you it was lame. Can I come in for a minute?"

"I guess." Heather flounced back on her bed, sitting Indian-style with a huge, fluffy stuffed cat hugged in her arms.

Such a contrast, Darcie thought. A little girl, surrounded by both little girl and grown-up trappings. There were posters of rock stars and movie idols and charcoal sketches of dolphins on the walls, perfume bottles and makeup pots on the dresser, a black bra draped over a chair, Winnie the Pooh flannel pajamas crumpled on the floor and ice skates draped over a freestanding full-length oval mirror. Overstuffed pillows decorated the purple-and-green comforter on the bed, vying for space with the myriad stuffed animals in all colors and sizes. An algebra book was nearly hidden by a wadded-up chenille throw in soft lilac.

Cushions in the same purple and green pattern as the bedspread curved along the sill of the bay window, a diary lying open there as though Heather had been staring wistfully out the window, watching the wind blow through the trees, recording both her little-girl and young-woman thoughts.

A tough time in a girl's life.

"Nice room," Darcie commented.

Heather shrugged. "Grandma helped me redo it. It used to be pink. But that was a baby color. I'll leave the pink for Mary Beth."

"Leave some for me, too. Half my apartment is done in pink."

Heather looked skeptical, disbelieving…intrigued. "Really?"

"Really. Actually, I call it peach. But Grandma calls it the pink house."

Heather grinned and buried her face in her stuffed cat. "I like your grandma."

"She likes you, too. That's one of the reasons I'm here. Ma and Grandma said you guys have to come back for dinner."

"You mean my whole family?"

"Yes."

Heather's expression resembled a snow cloud that had parted to allow a burst of sunshine. Then just as quickly, skepticism took hold, closing out the light. "My dad'll say no. He's got some stupid deadline he has to meet and he's supposed to go to that stupid Daddy Club thing tonight. And I bet he expects me to baby-sit—never mind that he hasn't even asked me. He never asks."

"That's not fair, is it?"

"Sometimes I get scared here by myself. What if

I do something wrong or..." She seemed to realize she was admitting to vulnerability and made a quick adjustment. "Or what if I wanted to go out? Maybe I have plans."

This was the attitude that had Flynn in such a tizzy. Darcie felt for him.

"Gee, I was hoping you didn't already have plans for tonight. Besides dinner at my folks' house, there's a class at Hardware and Muffins on fuse boxes and how to shut off gas valves. I figured I could learn something and not have to call my dad or my neighbors when we have a power outage. And I thought that maybe you'd like to sit in on it with me. It'll help you out those times you're by yourself."

"Yeah, which seems to be a lot lately," Heather grumbled, determined to keep up the pretense. She liked Darcie. And she liked hanging out with Darcie's family. And she sort of wanted to see what her dad was really doing at this Daddy Club gig. You never knew about these groups. They might be teaching him all the wrong kind of stuff.

It wasn't like her dad was a total nerd or anything. He was pretty cool most of the time, and she didn't want a bunch of rigid old men making him a whole lot different.

Then a thought struck. "If we...hang out, does that mean I can't call you at the hot line?" Was this a breach of ethics or something? "And are you gonna tell my dad?"

"You can still call me, Heather. Not just at the hot line, either. I'll give you my home number and my beeper and cell phone…and the number at my parents' house, as well. And what we talk about will be between us, okay?''

''Okay. Yeah. I'd like to have dinner at your house. Dad made grilled-cheese sandwiches twice this week and burned them both times. I mean, how hard can toasted cheese be?''

''Evidently next to impossible for some. But tonight I guarantee you've hit the suppertime jackpot. Change into some warm clothes. It's cold out there, and it looks like snow before the night's over.''

Feeling proud that she'd accomplished her goal with Heather, Darcie made her way back down the stairs, trailing her hand lightly over the mahogany banister of the curving staircase. Below and to the right were the living room and a massive fireplace with a beveled mirror that nearly reached the eighteen-foot-high vaulted ceiling.

With each step she took, her cranberry pantsuit reflected in the mirror, the sparkling glass tracking her progress down the staircase.

It made her feel a bit like Cinderella. Darcie Moretti, middle-class girl from the burg, actually inside her prince's castle in Princeton.

On impulse she struck a pose and raised an imaginary fan to her face, trying for both a sultry and coy look—perhaps a touch of elegance given the surroundings.

Foolish woman, she chided.

She took her gaze off the mirror…and it slammed right into Flynn's.

Startled, she gave a quick, typically feminine, one-note scream.

He stood below her, watching, grinning and holding his baby daughter with one strong arm.

Oh, the man could make her heart pound without even half trying.

Her face heated because she knew he'd seen her peacock act of admiring herself in the mirror. She imagined that he could read her mind, and that he knew of her fanciful thoughts.

Squaring her shoulders, she went down the rest of the steps with dispatch—despite the fact that she'd already given herself away by yelping.

This wasn't the first time somebody had caught her in the act of doing something stupid. That was the story of her life.

She came to a halt on the marble tiles in the foyer and looked him straight in the eyes. "What?" she challenged.

His grin widened, his brows lifting in mock innocence. "Nothing."

"That's what I thought." She automatically took Mary Beth from his arms—a distraction.

Okay, so she was a chicken.

And so she was more embarrassed than usual that Flynn O'Grady had caught her mugging in a mirror.

FLYNN WASN'T SURE why he'd accepted the Morettis' dinner invitation. He knew the minute it was extended that Darcie hadn't meant to offer. Perhaps that's why he'd agreed.

Besides, she intrigued him, made him feel

alive…and she was going to have his baby. He wanted to know why it had taken so long for her to even mention the situation to him.

And despite the difficulties he was currently having—and determined to get better at—he wanted that baby growing inside Darcie's womb. He would never abandon a child like his own father had, like his wife had.

The rain made the outside miserable, but inside Rose Moretti's kitchen he felt at home. "I hope this isn't too much trouble for you."

"Trouble?" Rose looked as though he'd suggested the world was square. "Nonsense. We have plenty. I tell Darcie she should invite nice company more often."

"She invites bad company?" he teased.

Rose smacked him lightly with her dish towel and giggled like a schoolgirl. "You are a bad one, Flynn O'Grady." She shoved a bowl of gravy in his hands. "Put that on the table and sit."

"Yes, ma'am."

"Bossy, isn't she?" Darcie said, settling Mary Beth in the high chair that the Morettis kept for their visiting grandchildren.

"Scary, I'm thinking." Flynn set the porcelain bowl on the table and nodded in Heather's direction. "Your mother's had her hopping since the minute we walked in the door. I've never seen Heather set the table without a fuss—and with a smile on her face."

"I don't think Ma will actually follow through with her threat of splinters under the fingernails."

Flynn's eyes widened and Darcie laughed. "I was kidding."

He flushed. "I knew that."

Rose bustled into the room carrying a roasted turkey on a platter. Flynn had his taste buds set for fried chicken, but this looked and smelled even better.

"Everyone sit. Johnny, you've met Darcie's friend Flynn and his sweet girls, yes?"

"Yes, Rosie." Johnny Moretti extended his hand to Flynn. "Good to have you join us."

"Do you carry a gun?" Grandma asked.

Flynn's lips twitched. He'd been warned about this conversation.

"Now, Edna..." Johnny began, only to be ignored.

"Well, it's a legitimate question." She looked at Flynn again. "Do you?"

"No."

"Pity. Those folks at the cable place need a good shaking up. I'll call my grandson." She sniffed and tugged at her fuchsia sweater that was draped over her shoulders.

Darcie had planned to sit next to Mary Beth—she needed the practice for when she had her own baby in a few months time—but her mother shooed her away, craftily maneuvering it so that she was sitting thigh to thigh with Flynn.

It was terribly distracting. Even more distracting than her grandmother's new hair color.

"Uh, Grandma, I like your hair."

Edna fluffed her wiry orange curls. "That nice

young Priscilla Vendette down at Shirley's Beauty Shop did it.''

The color was atrocious. It looked like Priscilla Vendette had a *vendetta* against Grandma.

''It's very nice.''

Flynn bumped her leg with his. She bit her lip, gave him a look that clearly said, ''She's a grandma. She's entitled to look like a walking fashion disaster.''

''My friend did her hair like that,'' Heather said. ''Except she put pink stripes in the front.''

Flynn cringed.

''Do tell,'' Grandma said, bobbing her head. ''Maybe I'll get me some of those stripes next time. 'Course it's a wonder I didn't get them naturally when I came within inches of being stomped to death by a wild turkey. It was enough to turn even a young woman's hair white—or pink in my case,'' she said, cutting her gaze to Heather.

''A wild turkey?'' Heather asked, her eyes round.

''A huge beast.''

''Now, Mother—''

''Were you there?'' Grandma demanded, her look shooting daggers at Darcie's mom.

Rose put a spoonful of yams on her plate and passed the bowl.

''Liked to have killed me dead, he did,'' Grandma said, thrilled to have Heather as a rapt audience and playing it to the hilt. ''I'm an old woman and my heart's not what it used to be.''

Darcie's parents exchanged a look that silently

shouted, ''Give me a break.'' Grandma Connor passed the green beans and didn't bat an eye.

''What happened?'' Heather was truly awed. Just as Grandma Connor knew she'd be.

''Gave me a fright, is what happened. I was taking my morning walk like I always do, and big as you please, this turkey came charging right at me with malicious intent in his beady eyes. Don't know what the world's coming to. Deer running wild in the streets of Princeton and now the turkeys helping themselves to folks' gardens and scaring old ladies half to death.''

Heather giggled and Mary Beth joined in, banging her spoon on the wooden tray of the high chair.

Flynn's lips twitched. It did his heart good to see his daughters happy. And it was Darcie's doing because she'd brought them here. She'd been right about her mother and grandmother's effect on Heather.

Grandma Connor fluffed her orange curls, making her hairdo worse. ''Tell you what, I'm not taking my morning constitutional again unless I'm packin' a piece.''

Darcie put her hand on Flynn's thigh and leaned close. ''Don't pay her any mind,'' she whispered.

He wasn't sure he could draw a breath, much less use his mind. The feel of her palm high on his thigh totally derailed his brain. His emotions were on a roller coaster. Desirous, cautious, peaceful, back to uneasy, then shooting off in a direction that scared him to death.

"Grandma, it's against the law to carry concealed weapons."

"Humph." In a mortifying switch of conversational gears—a talent of Grandma Connor's—she turned back to Flynn. "Heather says you don't have any tattoos. Is that right?"

"Grandma," Darcie warned, knowing where this was going and helpless to stop it.

"Well, I can ask," Edna said. "A daughter wouldn't know if maybe her daddy had one on his private parts. Like you do, Darcie."

This, at last, got a reaction out of Johnny. His palm hit the table, making the silverware jump. "You've got a tattoo?" he roared.

"Yep. Right on her butt."

"It's not on my butt! It's on my hip."

"Same difference."

"When did you get a tattoo?" Johnny asked again.

"A long time ago, Daddy. Shirley Rogers dared me and promised to get one too. And then she backed out. I'm still gonna get her for it, you wait and see. That sucker hurt like the devil!"

There were several beats of silence after her admission. She noticed that Flynn was staring at her with a seriously intrigued look on his face. It had been dark in the hotel room. She'd wondered if he'd seen the tattoo and just not commented. Now she had her answer. He didn't know about the little sunflower. But his look said that he definitely wanted to.

Heather, too, was staring, but her expression was

one of worship. *Uh-oh,* Darcie thought. This could spell trouble. Next thing, Heather would want one, too.

Typical for the Moretti clan, everyone began talking at once, each perfectly able to juggle a minimum of three conversational balls at once. Not that anybody was truly listening to anybody else.

Thankfully Flynn and his girls were distracted, watching this skill with a combination of awe and disbelief. Darcie figured they'd had enough for one evening.

She stood and grabbed her plate, and then grabbed Flynn's too, even though he still had his fork in his hand. "We've got to be going. We'll be late for class."

"What class is that, dear?" Rose popped up to clear more dishes, obviously happy to change the direction and the temperature of this free-for-all conversation.

"Flynn's going to a Daddy Club meeting, and Heather and I are going to the Women in Hardware KoffeeKlatch. Tonight it's circuit breakers and gas valves."

"Nothing like a good shot of electricity to curl a girl's hair," Grandma said to no one in particular, guarding the bowl of sweet potatoes with one hand and brandishing a fork in the other.

"Does your brother know about this tattoo?" Johnny demanded, obviously not yet ready to drop the subject. "Why am I the last to know that my own daughter has mutilated her body?"

"I didn't mutilate my body, Daddy." She came

around the table and kissed him on the head. "And little John doesn't know." It seemed so silly to call her six-foot-three-inch brother "little." She plucked Mary Beth out of the high chair. "Thanks for dinner, Ma. Up you go, Heather. We've gotta book or we'll be late."

"But you haven't had dessert," Rose exclaimed as though this could cause the nation to crumble. "You'll at least take home a dish."

Darcie wanted to get out of here. Wanted to be safely in her car. Hopefully, by the time they reached Hardware and Muffins, Flynn would've forgotten this conversation. He would have stopped looking at her like he wanted her to strip right here and show him that darn tattoo...and other parts, too.

It was a hungry look no man should be giving her in her mother's dining room. Never mind that the man was the father of her baby.

"I don't have time to wait for you to wrap anything up, Ma."

"You have two minutes. Johnny, you tell her she has two minutes to wait for her mother." Rose pulled out empty containers, and heaped in enough leftovers to last a month. "And Flynn will take some home, too. A man needs a woman to cook for him."

"Oh, please, Ma. He can cook for himself."

"No, he can't," Heather said.

"Thanks for the vote of confidence, kiddo," Flynn looped his arm around Heather's neck, a pleased look on his face when she snuggled into him.

"This will help out," Rose said, loading plastic

bowls into a shopping bag and handing it to Heather. "You get those in the fridge as soon as you get home. Or better yet, why don't you leave the baby here with me and come back for her and the dishes after your class?"

"No!" Darcie's voice was so sharp, everyone in the room looked her way.

"Thank you for the offer, Mrs. Moretti," Flynn said easily, "but the class is closer to where I live." But not by much. He took his arm from around Heather so she could go retrieve their coats from the front bedroom.

"Oh, of course. It would be out of your way."

"That's not to say we can't baby-sit sometime," Grandma said. "You being a single man and all, you might want to go out on a date or two. And our Darcie's a single girl, too. You kids might want to hook up." Edna hitched up her black stretch pants where they were bagging at the knee. "Did I tell you my granddaughter's a married lady?"

Flynn looked at Darcie. "She is?"

"Not Darcie. The other one. Her sister, Celia. Got a couple of cute kids, too. Lives over in Connecticut with her lawyer husband. Come to think of it, we don't have an architect in the family, now do we, Rosie?"

Flynn began to sweat. Did they know he was Darcie's baby's father? It didn't appear so. And it made him feel like a louse. He'd accepted what Darcie had offered five months ago, never thinking of the consequences. And now she was bearing those consequences. Alone.

And why didn't he know about Darcie's tattoo? He ought to be shot. A man should take his time with a woman, worship her body, notice every sweet inch.

Now, more than ever, he had a burning desire to remedy that oversight, to see and taste and touch every part of Darcie Moretti, from the inside out, slowly, thoroughly....

Darcie saw the hungry look on Flynn's face and nearly died. If she could see it, so could everybody else. They needed to get out of here. Fast. No wonder Grandma Connor was hinting about welcoming architects into the family. Flynn O'Grady looked like he was game.

She shook her head, knowing her cheeks were bright red. "Cut it out, Grandma."

"Watch that smart mouth, girl. You respect your elders."

Darcie kissed her grandmother on the cheek. "Yeah, yeah. You're a menace but I love you." She tugged at Flynn's sleeve. "We gotta go." She didn't want her family putting him on the spot. Already her parents were sending speculative looks between Flynn and her pregnant belly.

"Wait!" Rose said, rushing forward with half a cake in each of her hands. "You kids split this dessert between you."

"I'll be big as a house!"

"Why does she always give away my dessert?" Johnny grumbled.

Rose ignored her husband. "Nonsense. You'll be healthy, keep up your strength for that baby." She hugged and kissed each one of them in turn, clucking like a mother hen.

Darcie watched Heather's reaction, saw the instant stiffening, then the inevitable yearning as her young arms went around Rose's girth and hugged.

Throat aching, Darcie looked away. So many memories were wrapped up in her mother's arms; so many hurts had been soothed. Even when she'd announced her pregnancy, but refused to name the father or the circumstances, there had been arms to hold her.

She was so very lucky to still have her mother to hug her. Heather didn't have that luxury.

And the hurt Darcie could see still stamped on the young girl's face wasn't something that would go away just because somebody wished it.

She'd seen Heather's nervous glances when Flynn laughed a little louder or leaned in too close to Darcie. It made her realize there was little hope of Heather accepting much more than a Wednesday-night supper from a Moretti. She wouldn't welcome the addition of another woman and child in her life.

Just like Tammy had never accepted a new woman in hers.

Darcie kept imagining fairy tale endings for herself, when it should be Heather and her welfare that were paramount.

She ran her hand over her swollen tummy, getting butterflies in her stomach when she thought of the baby growing inside her womb. She wished things could have been different. And she was going to stop that pity party right now. Grandma Connor always said baying at the moon was for coyotes and poets. And since Darcie was neither, she was wasting time.

Chapter Six

It only took twenty minutes to get from her parents' house to Hardware and Muffins. She parked her car beside Flynn's Suburban and got out to help him with the kids.

Heather had already dashed to the sidewalk to beat the rain.

Darcie hid a grin as Flynn juggled car keys, a coat and diaper bag while fiddling with the car seat.

"Here, let me take something," she offered, trying to relieve him of the diaper bag.

"You shouldn't be lifting." His gaze went to her stomach.

"Who in the world told you that?"

He shrugged and then dodged when she again tried to ease his load. "I've got it, Darc."

"There's no need to be so stubborn."

"I've got to learn this stuff, get more comfortable with doing it on my own. That's half the reason I'm attending these Daddy Club classes."

As he straightened, he conked his head on the car

door and barely gave a grimace, a clear indication that he'd done this several times before.

Darcie automatically reached up and pulled Mary Beth's pink hood over her head.

"Thanks."

The heat in his gaze was almost her undoing. She joined Heather on the sidewalk, determined to put distance between herself and sexy Flynn O'Grady.

"We're early," Darcie said. "What do you say we get some caffe mocha and biscotti? Or just a good hot cup of chocolate."

Heather's eyes widened. "We just had supper."

"Okay, *I'll* have coffee and biscotti. Or maybe one of Ruth Naomi's apricot muffins."

Flynn caught up with them. "Woman, you just ate."

"That's what I said," Heather agreed with a giggle.

"Fine." Darcie pushed open the door. "I defy both of you to smell this wonderful aroma and resist."

Holding Mary Beth, Flynn managed to put his other arm around both Darcie and Heather and urge them indoors. He nearly tripped over his own feet when he saw the larger-than-normal crowd inside Hardware and Muffins.

"Whoa, what's all this?"

"The ladies' class is meeting tonight, too, remember?"

"Won't that be a bit of a conflict? How are we going to separate ourselves?" Already he was feeling intimidated. Admitting to his shortcomings in front of a bunch of guys was humiliating, but at least it was better than doing it in front of a group of women, too.

Ruth Naomi bustled over, sweeping Heather under her arm. "Excellent! Young people. Come right this way, lamb. And you, too," she cooed, scooping Mary Beth out of Flynn's arms. "Glad you could make it, Flynn, Darcie. Hell of a storm moving in, huh?"

Flynn had to get used to women blazing right over him. First the Morettis, now Mrs. Steadwell. Still a bit overwhelmed, he hovered by the door, seriously considering the merits of bolting. Instead, he took off his coat, watching as Ruth Naomi disappeared behind the bakery cases and into the kitchen with his children. Combining a hardware store with a designer coffee and dessert bar was an ingenious idea.

"The ladies don't usually meet on Wednesdays?" he asked, picking up the thread of their conversation.

"Uh-uh. But Ula Mae chartered a bus to Atlantic City, and since half of these ladies here are going with her—it's their monthly gambling run—there was a conflict. So Ross is going to teach us girls about fuse boxes, and Terrence is going to discuss nutrition with you guys—and he'll give you cooking pointers to boot. Since he's a chef by trade, he won't be able to help himself," she said, grinning.

"How do you know all this?"

"I'm in the loop."

He raised his brows, indicating she should elaborate.

"One of my accounts is Data, Ink., where Elaine

Baransky works—whoops, she's a Steadwell now. I keep forgetting. Though I don't know how. The way Ross looks at her is enough to burn the memory into most anybody's mind.''

"And Elaine told you about the change?'' Flynn was having a hard time concentrating on Darcie's story. Those two freckles at the side of her mouth fascinated him, distracted him.

"No. Ula Mae told me. I handle some investments for her, as well as her extended health care policy. By the way, how are you fixed for insurance?''

He shook his head. "For a woman who's painfully direct, you can be scattered, can't you?'' She absolutely charmed him.

"My mind goes a thousand miles an hour. It feels like I've always got way more to do than I have time to do it in.''

"Another thing we have in common,'' he said. Though it gave him a twinge. Two overwhelmed people in the same household didn't work well. He knew that for sure. That had been the crux of the problem in his marriage to Marsha.

Flynn followed Darcie's gaze and smiled at the sight of the women fawning over the girls. Despite Heather's claim of being full, Ruth Naomi had urged a muffin into her hand. The women were giving equal time to the girls, keeping them both occupied.

"So, you're pretty well fixed for insurance?'' Darcie was back on their earlier topic. "Need any financial advice? Additional health or life packages?''

"I've got plenty."

She shrugged. "It never hurts to get a comparison. I can work you up something if you like— Oh!"

"What?" He nearly shouted it, was next to her in a flash. "What's wrong?"

"The baby kicked." Not thinking, she automatically grabbed his hand and placed it on her belly, tugging him out of immediate sight behind a bin of power tools.

The intimacy was immediate and exquisitely profound. Their gazes locked and clung. The worry in his eyes softened to something incredibly personal.

For no good reason, tears sprang to her eyes. Astonished, embarrassed, she looked away. She hadn't realized how much she craved this touch, this sharing.

With a gentle caress of his fingertips against her chin, Flynn turned her face to his. "Oh, baby, don't." He pulled her to him, forgetting they were in a crowded hardware store, albeit between the aisles. "Shh, don't cry. Please." God, this made him a nervous wreck. "I don't know what to do when women cry."

Darcie laughed and sniffed. "Typical. Are you this way when Heather spouts like a watering pot?"

"'Fraid so."

The baby wasn't through frolicking—or else she was responding to Darcie's emotions. Pressed against Flynn's stomach, there was no way he couldn't feel the miracle of the child moving in her womb.

Afraid of the intimacy, of the bittersweet agony of wanting something she couldn't have, Darcie stepped back.

"I'm okay now. This happens at the weirdest times. I should just forget eye makeup altogether for the rest of my pregnancy."

"Do you regret the baby?"

The question came out of nowhere. There were so many things she longed to share with him—like the baby moving in her womb, or the sonogram film that was proudly displayed in a plastic photo holder in her wallet. But they were in a hardware store filled with people. "Now isn't the time to go into this."

"Marsha didn't want Mary Beth." His hands were shoved in his pockets, the diaper bag still draped over his shoulder. And his sad gaze was fixed across the room—on his daughters.

"Oh, Flynn, I'm sorry." *Never mind the timing,* she thought. "And no, I don't regret the baby. Sure I wish the circumstances were different, but they're not. And I'm okay with it. I'm also happy and awed by this baby and the changes she's bringing to my body."

"It's true that pregnant woman have a special glow," he said softly. "You've got it."

The intensity of his look made her squirm. She needed to lighten up the conversation. "That's just the freckles glowing from the cold."

He ran a finger down her cheek, over her lips, his gaze steady on hers. "I like your freckles."

"Flynn," she warned, her heart slamming against

her chest, her good intentions a breath away from crumbling. Sex wasn't their problem. The chemistry between them was explosive. It was all the other stuff that got in their way.

"What?" Slowly, reluctantly it seemed, his eyes lifted to hers.

"You're going to get us in trouble."

"Seems like I already did that. Would a repeat performance be so bad?"

"Yes. It would. You've got a Daddy Club meeting to attend, and I'm supposed to be learning about fuses."

"There's plenty of electricity going on right here between us."

"All the more reason I need to learn how to shut it off."

"It's not as easy as flipping a circuit breaker, Darc."

"That's what I'm afraid of. But I'm going to do it anyway." She looked around the aisle, noticed that Ula Mae was watching them shrewdly and realized that they weren't as hidden as she'd thought.

Thank goodness Ruth Naomi was distracting Heather. It wouldn't be a good idea for the girl to see her father fooling around with a woman.

It was clear from her conversations with Heather over the hot line that the teen's emotions were still raw from losing her mother.

And the girl did *not* want a replacement.

HALFWAY THROUGH the instruction on nutrition, Ross Steadwell joined The Daddy Club group and sat next to Flynn.

"I thought you were teaching circuit breakers," Flynn said.

"I was. But the ladies got bored. Said that was too easy and they got it the first time. They were more interested in stock quotes and financial advice from Darcie. So she's taken over the class."

Sure enough, the ladies were huddled around Darcie. She had her laptop computer powered on. Flynn frowned.

"Where'd she get the computer?"

"Brought it with her."

"No. I came with her. She didn't have a computer in her hand."

"She had it in her car. She always has it with her."

"How do you know?"

"Who do you think we get all our financial advice from? Darcie's a whiz. And she's dead-on with her predictions."

"I thought she sold insurance." Why did the idea of her being a Wall Street wizard bother him?

"That, too. But Darcie's got a knack for giving sound investment advice. She's doubled and tripled a lot of these people's pension funds. I wonder how she finds the time to fit it all in. She's one busy lady. And sweet. If I weren't a married man, I'd make a play for her myself." Ross leaned an elbow on his knee. "Heard about your troubles with Heather. Things getting any better on that front?"

"It's hard to tell." Man alive, did everybody

know what a failure he was becoming? "That girl has mood swings worse than...well, they're pretty bad. I can't seem to keep up."

"If anybody can straighten her out, Darcie can. She's had an excellent success rate at that hot line she runs."

"Heather shouldn't need to be calling a hot line. You know me, Ross. I'm not such a bad guy. Why can't she come to me?"

"Don't know, man. Leave it to Darcie, though. She's fierce about that hot line. And she's fierce about the kids. She'll sacrifice anything for a teen in need. Like I said, she's special. I tell you what, though. I'd sure like to get my hands on the jerk who got her pregnant and left her high and dry."

Aw, hell. "Uh...what makes you think the guy dumped her?"

Ross's gaze jerked to Flynn, a muscle in his jaw tensing. "Do you see a ring on her finger?"

"There could be a good reason why the guy doesn't step forward." His voice was a whispery rasp. He felt bad enough. He didn't want the rest of the group overhearing. Or, God forbid, he didn't want Darcie and her women's group overhearing. Granted, Darcie was wrong for waiting so long to tell him about the baby, but he had to take responsibility, too, because he'd helped her create that baby. Still, the two of them needed time to talk and work out their relationship before he made any confessions to his friend.

Ross gave him a speculative look. "You said you

came with Darcie tonight. I didn't realize the two of you were dating.''

"We aren't.'' That sounded awful. Then again, Ross didn't know he was the jerk they'd been talking about. "We ran into each other at that architect convention I went to several months back. Evidently there was an insurance one going on at the same time. We had a drink together, and then…well, she didn't give me her phone number or address, or anything. I assumed she lived over in Philly. I had no idea she was right here practically in my back yard.''

From across the room, Flynn watched Darcie explaining something to her group of onlookers. She took her fingers off the laptop keys, her expression animated and her arms waving in the air as though putting extra emphasis on her words. She shook her head, and sent a silent apology with her gaze to Myrna Jawoski when her exuberance nearly knocked over the older lady's latte.

A woman who talks with her hands, he thought. Passionate. Volatile. A man's fantasy. She'd definitely been his.

And she could well be the answer to his prayers. He noted how close his daughter stood to Darcie, lapping up the company and the attention, trying— and failing—to look nonchalant.

But Ross's comment about Darcie being super busy hit an off-key chord inside him. Marsha had been overwhelmingly busy. And she'd loved what she did—her work. Loved it more than she'd loved them. He'd talked her into staying long enough to have Mary Beth, hoping she'd realize that family was important, that *he* was important. But none of them had stood a chance against her love of her job as a marketing executive for a Fortune 100 company. She'd left them, told him her attorney would serve the divorce papers...but a delivery van on a crowded Manhattan street had failed to heed a red light and Marsha had become his *late* wife before she could have her way and become his *ex* wife.

"Looks like there's more to you two than you're saying," Ross said.

Flynn jolted like a teen who'd been caught peeping in the girl's locker room at school. He wondered if his friend would take a poke at him if he admitted just how much more there was. "I care about her."

"And you cared about her at that convention.... When was that? About five months ago?"

He clenched his teeth, considered not answering. But Ross's expression made it clear he'd already put two and two together. "I didn't know," Flynn said quietly.

"And now you do."

"It's not that simple," Flynn said. "Darcie's a hard one to pin down. When I bring up the subject of the baby, she puts me off. I tried calling her all last week, but she went out of town. Then out of the blue she showed up at my house tonight. We haven't had a chance to be alone to discuss anything. I'd have forgone this Daddy Club meeting, but she wouldn't hear of it."

"So you intend to do right by her?"

''Hell, Ross, you sound like her brother or something.''

''Now there's where you'll have a big problem,'' Ross said with a mock shudder. ''If Johnny Moretti hears about you, he'll shoot first and ask questions later.''

''I've already met Johnny Moretti.''

''The brother?''

''No. The dad.''

''And he knows you're the one who got her pregnant?''

''Would you quit saying it like that?''

''Like what?'' Ross asked, all innocence.

''Like I did this on purpose or something.''

Ross raised a brow. ''Guess you'll be attending the class on condoms next, huh?''

Flynn shook his head, ignoring his friend's dig, determined to bring the conversation back under control. ''Darcie didn't tell her family.'' And that bugged him, too.

''Take my advice. When you own up to your responsibility, wear armor.''

''Hell, her brother can't be that bad.''

''Just trust me, wear the armor. In the meantime, it looks like you're more in need of parenting instruction than we thought.'' Shoving up his sleeves, Ross stood. ''Let's go let Terrence teach us how to make crepes. We'll be the envy of every Mr. Mom in the state.''

''Are you kidding? I doubt I'll ever graduate to anyone's envy. I can't even handle toasted cheese with any sort of credibility.''

"That's because you've had people taking care of you for too much of your life. It's time for you to be the one to take care now, buddy."

Flynn stood and shoved his hands in the pockets of his zip-front sweatshirt. "What is this? Pick-on-Flynn night?"

Ross laughed and thumped him on the back. "Just think of all the character you're building."

BUILDING CHARACTER.

The words came back to haunt him the following day. If he built any more character, he was going to wig out.

He shut the door behind the social worker and leaned his forehead on the oak jamb, his heart beating like a jackhammer.

He felt sick, his gut twisted in knots. He didn't know which way to turn, or to where.

Before he knew what he intended, his hand was on the phone, his fingers stabbing at numbers. The first try got him Darcie's answering machine.

The second got her voice mail.

He swore, and punched in her pager number, then sat with his hand clutching the portable telephone, absently noting how the tendons were standing out on his arm. He wondered if they were doing the same on his neck.

He also wondered how often fathers were committed to insane asylums—or checked themselves in on a purely voluntary basis.

The shrill ring of the phone made him jump like a guilty convict. He stabbed the talk button, didn't bother waiting to see who was on the line. "I need help."

A pause, then Darcie's voice. "Are you okay? Is it the girls? Is someone hurt?"

"Wait! I'm sorry. I didn't mean to scare you. But damn it, Darcie, I don't know what to do."

"Tell me what's wrong."

"I just had a visit from Social Services."

"Social… They came to the house?"

"Yes."

"Where's Mary Beth?"

"Upstairs. Napping."

"Okay. I'll be right there."

The phone went dead before he could say another word. That she would rush to his side made him feel better, special, like she cared. God, he hadn't realized how sketchy he'd gotten lately about people caring.

Taking the stairs two at a time, he went to check on Mary Beth and pulled the pink blanket up to her chubby little chin, careful not to wake her. She was a petite baby, looking more like six months than twelve. So different than Heather had been at that age.

Funny how clearly he remembered Heather as a baby. He'd thought he was rusty, that his memories were faulty. But he did remember…her toddling steps, her big blue eyes turned on him as though he were her giant savior, the first time she'd called him Da-Da. But what had he really given her in return? He'd been so busy trying to get ahead, and he'd left the raising of his daughter to Marsha, who in turn had eventually handed over that responsibility to a nanny.

He ran his hand lightly over Mary Beth's curls. Things were going to be different from now on. He was going to learn to be a good father if it killed him.

And if Heather had her way, it just might.

When he was halfway down the stairs, there was a desperate banging on the door.

He opened the door and Darcie whooshed in, bringing in cold air and the scent of her apple pie perfume.

Just seeing her made his chest tighten and his gut fill with butterflies. She was his ally; she felt so familiar…so right. She was his anchor in a turbulent storm.

He needed her.

"We need to get married."

Chapter Seven

Darcie stopped dead at his abrupt words. Then she simply ignored him, taking off her gloves and scarf and unbuttoning her coat. "So what happened here?"

"Did you hear me?"

"Of course I heard you. But I generally ignore crazy people. Tell me what Social Services wanted."

Flynn sighed. He hadn't meant to blurt that marriage demand, but it was a good suggestion. Darcie was having his baby. He wanted to take responsibility for her. He cared about her. And he needed support. He was scared. Scared of parenting by himself. Scared of failing—with the two girls he had as well as the one yet to be born.

With Darcie by his side, he would be strong. She had a way of infusing strength and peace into those whose lives she touched. And God, he wanted her to touch his.

"Evidently Heather was talking to some kids at

school and she told them that I left without taking Mary Beth with me—"

"Left where?"

"I don't know. The only thing I can think is the other night, before The Daddy Club—the incident you walked into the middle of. I needed to make some quick copies of a set of blueprints."

"Heather *is* old enough to baby-sit, Flynn."

"I know. And I've never left Mary Beth alone. For that matter, I rarely leave Heather on her own. But I guess Heather made it sound like I do."

"Young people tend to exaggerate."

"Yeah, well my daughter exaggerated us right into a visit by Social Services."

"And what did they say?"

"That they'll keep their eye on me." At Darcie's frown, he said, "Well, they actually said they could see that everything appeared fine here, but they still want to talk to Heather." He paced away. "Hell, Darcie, I'm going to have a record, be on file at some county office for anybody and everybody to see and speculate on!"

"I doubt that it'll come to that."

He didn't seem to hear her. "They were headed over to the school to talk to Heather, but I told them her class went on a field trip today to Princeton University."

"Did they? Or was that just an excuse to stall them?"

"Of course they went. I'm not such a terrible father that I don't keep up with what my daughter's doing."

"Nobody said you were a terrible father, Flynn."

"Are you kidding? My daughter calls a runaway hot line and brings Social Services down on my head. A woman I've been intimate with conspires with my friends to get me to attend a class for hapless dads. I've burned every damned thing in the kitchen—twice at least—and Mary Beth's T-shirts are all pink!"

Darcie glanced down at his socks, realizing that it hadn't been a trick of the light. One of his socks *was* a different color. "Pink's a good color for little girls."

"Little girls maybe. You try facing a thirteen-year-old and explaining how her skintight white sweater turned pink."

"Skintight, huh?"

"Yes, it's no loss, really. I hated that sweater. What does she need with her belly hanging out in the dead of winter anyway?"

"But that's beside the point, right?" Darcie figured it wouldn't be a good idea to smile right about now. The poor guy was up to his ears, and sinking fast. Besides, this was truly a grave situation, one that could easily go bad. Darcie had seen that happen too many times to take for granted.

"What time will Heather's class be back?"

He glanced at his watch. "Probably in another half hour or so. I hate the thought of those people waiting for her like a bunch of secret agents or something, of them pulling her out of class and scaring her like that."

"Do you want to go pick her up? Sit in with her while they talk to her?"

"Like they're going to let me listen in on their questions," he said with a touch of sarcasm. "I still don't think they're convinced I'm okay. Hell, Darcie, they looked in the cupboards like I was starving my kids or something."

She put her hand on his arm. "I'll stay here with Mary Beth. You go pick up your daughter and take some time to talk to her."

He looked like she'd just offered him the moon then snatched it back again. "Heather and I don't do well in the talking department lately."

"Then it's time to change that, isn't it?"

"Yeah. It is." He cupped her face, tunneled his fingers through her thick mass of hair and looked at her, his gaze intent, questions in his brown eyes. Slowly he leaned in, as though to kiss her.

Darcie's heart thudded and it became difficult to draw a breath. At the last second she put her hand between them, her fingers over his lips. "Don't."

He frowned and stared at her for a long moment. "I need to go see about Heather. But when I get back, we're going to talk about us, Darcie."

"Is that a threat?"

"Take it any way you want. You're having my baby. And I want you to marry me."

She stepped back, fighting the ache in her throat. It seemed she'd waited all her life to hear those words from Flynn O'Grady. But she'd always imagined them attached to declarations of love, too.

And never had she thought the well-being of a teen would be between them.

"When you talk to Heather, try to let her take the conversational lead. You have a tendency to make demands that are easy to misconstrue."

"You think wanting to marry you because you're having my baby is too strong of a demand?"

"If it means losing Heather, then absolutely, yes, I do."

Lose Heather? That didn't make sense. But Flynn was too anxious to see his daughter to pursue the topic further. And he knew darn well, marrying Darcie would silence a lot of his problems.

He just wasn't sure if marriage would create new ones.

FLYNN WATCHED DARCIE with his daughters. Heather was all apologetic over her dramatically embellished comments at school that had brought Social Services down on their heads. Liz Holland, the girl who ratted, was on Heather's fink list and no longer considered a friend. Flynn figured that attitude would last about a week.

Totally contrite, Heather had hopped right up after dinner to do the dishes and even offered to give Mary Beth a bath—all without a hint of her trademark rolling of the eyes.

Darcie had Mary Beth hitched on her hip and stood by Heather's side at the sink, assisting with the dishes one-handed. That's when Flynn realized he was just sitting there like a lump on a log, letting them do all the work by themselves.

He stood to clear the rest of the dishes, but paused when he heard Darcie's laugh. He hadn't been paying attention to their conversation, but he loved the sound of her laugh, loved the way his daughters joined in. Heather's giggle was high-pitched and Mary Beth's was the fun squeal of a baby that would invite the worst sourpuss to smile.

And though Flynn was by no means a sourpuss, his smile was spontaneous and unavoidable. Sidetracked, he just stood there and watched. Darcie was so good with his kids; she made it look so easy.

He wanted her to turn that attention on him. Because when the day was over and night shifted in, when quiet reigned and the kids were snug in their beds, the loneliness set in. He'd spent many a night listening to the clock ticking on the nightstand.

He needed conversation, intimacy, pillow talk.... Someone he could trust to stay—unconditionally.

His dad had walked out on them when he was a teen. Marsha had walked out after twelve years of marriage. At all stages of his life, people had abandoned him. What was lacking in him to cause this?

He didn't realize he was still standing there, staring, holding a bowl of mashed potatoes in one hand and two glasses in the other. Then Darcie turned around, her smile dimming just a bit, turning to compassion as though she could read his thoughts.

Did he look like a needy person or something?

Then her eyes softened and took on a look that any man would recognize.

Interest. Desire.

Now *this* he could handle. Darcie Moretti was attracted to him. That put him ahead of the game. And by God, he really was determined to get a look at that tattoo.

She held out her hand. "Did you want me to take those, or were you waiting for the dog to lick them clean?"

"We don't have a dog," Heather said.

"I know, hon. I was teasing your dad."

"That's right. Gang up on me." He stepped around Darcie. Ignoring her outstretched hand, he put the bowl under the running water, taking the opportunity to place a quick kiss on his daughter's hair, then turned and treated Mary Beth to the same. Just for the heck of it, to test the waters, he impulsively did the same to Darcie.

She drew in a swift breath, her gaze darting to Heather. But Heather had already turned back to the dishes. Still, Darcie's cheeks reddened, making her freckles stand out.

He got to her. Leaning close to her ear, he said, "I'll wear you down."

She gave him a look of warning, frustration evident that she couldn't comment because of Heather.

Flynn grinned and plucked Mary Beth out of Darcie's arms. "Time for this one's bath."

"I can do it, Daddy."

"You're doing dishes. I'll do the bath. Teamwork, right, kiddo?"

Guilt caused her to look away. "Yeah. I'm sorry," she whispered.

He put his arm around her, touched when Mary Beth reached out to pat her sister's hair as though she realized this was a tough moment. He was touched even more when he saw the tears spring to Darcie's eyes. His own eyes stung and his throat ached with emotion.

This could be a family—him, the girls, Darcie…and the new baby to come.

"No need to apologize again, widget." Tears tracked down Heather's cheeks when he used his pet name for her. "We're going to make it just fine." He wished Darcie would ease into their circle. He didn't have a free hand to pull her there. But she was a part of them, too. "We'll all be just fine."

FLYNN HEARD the doorbell ring, started to ignore it and then remembered that his mom wasn't here to answer it. He'd talked to her just this morning, telling her about their ordeal with Social Services yesterday. She'd offered to come back, but Aunt Lois still needed care with her broken hip, and Flynn was determined to stand on his own. He was serious about this Mr. Mom business. But right now, Mr. Mom needed to make some headway on these blueprints.

The computer-enhanced wall he was resizing with the design program went streaking across the screen like a comet when he heard Heather scream.

He leaped up, scattering pencils and rulers and knocked his keyboard askew. Ignoring the computer's incessant beeping that warned his keyboard was about to perform a fatal error, he charged toward the front door, his heart hammering like crazy, his protective instincts preparing him for fight.

It took him a moment to clear the haze from his vision, to realize that Heather was smiling and hopping around like a demented, deliriously happy person.

And that Darcie was standing at the door.

"What the hell—?"

"Look, Daddy! A kitten! Isn't she just the sweetest thing you ever saw? Can we keep her? Please?"

He noticed that Darcie wouldn't quite meet his gaze for a moment, and when she did, there wasn't an ounce of apology in her expression for bringing over a pet without getting his permission first.

His mouth pulled into a grin. His heart-pounding terror turned into something else entirely.

"Say yes, Daddy."

He dragged his gaze back to Heather's. How could he resist the plea in her eyes, the little girl happiness? Hell, even the cat was begging with its cute expression and huge blue eyes.

"She's got eyes the color of yours," he said to Heather, running his palm over the soft fur of the tiny white-and-gray kitten.

"See! It's an omen. Oh, baby kitty, you'll love it here! Thanks, Darcie! Thanks, Daddy!" She took off upstairs, talking nonsense to the kitten and pointing out the sights in the house as she went.

"Guess I said yes," he mumbled. His gaze turned back to Darcie.

"I know I should have checked with you first, but—"

He put a finger over her lips, melting her bones. "You did good, Darc."

"I'm glad." Lord, was that really her voice, all breathy and Mae West-like?

"So, the kitten's moving in. How about you?" he asked, urging her inside, closing the door slowly, all the while keeping his gaze on her, standing close, making her yearn.

She cleared her throat. "I take up a bit more room than a cat."

"I'm more than willing to share my room. Marry me, Darcie."

"I—I better get the kitty's supplies out of my car."

"I'll do it. Later." His hands tightened on the lapels of her coat.

"No. I need some air. I'm hot—"

"And bothered?"

The pupils of his eyes turned the deep brown irises nearly black. His warm breath bathed her face, caressed her mouth. She licked her lips. "If you must know, yes. So be nice and step aside."

He tsked softly. "Marry me, Darcie Moretti."

She stepped back, shook her head. "I'm kind of funny, ya know? Old-fashioned, if you can believe it." Especially in light of being pregnant out of wedlock—and resisting that proposal of wedded bliss. "I need to marry for love, not a baby."

She'd left him speechless. A clue that she'd made the right choice by turning him down. Besides, there was his daughter to think of. Allowing a kitten in her life might make the young girl happy, but that was a sweet furry animal. Totally different than inviting a stepmom into the fold.

"How do you know love's not involved?" he asked after a few beats.

"You don't know me well enough to love me." It hurt to admit that. She'd had a lifetime to fall for him, to build him up in her mind. She didn't imagine he'd ever even given her a second thought.

"I know you pretty well." His lingering glance at her belly spoke volumes.

"Anybody can have sex with somebody else without knowing them. That doesn't equate to a marriage."

"Then give us a chance. Move in here."

"Flynn, you have two impressionable daughters. Heather isn't ready for another woman to move into her life."

"She's coming around. Didn't you see how happy she was?"

"For goodness' sake, you should know by now that a teen's happy mood can shift in a matter of milliseconds."

"She's going to have to accept this sooner or later. You're having my baby, Darcie."

"Flynn—"

"No, don't shush me. She's upstairs playing with the kitten. She won't overhear us." He pulled her close, placed his palm on her poochy tummy. "This is our baby. Her sister. She's got to be told."

"I'm not ready." Heck, it took her months to get up the nerve to tell *him*. She clearly wasn't a woman to be rushed.

"Waiting won't change the situation."

"I know."

He smoothed the hair back from her face. "I care about you, Darcie. I need you in my life."

"*Need* me?"

"And *want* you."

She shook her head. "There's a lot of variables here. It might not be up to us."

"Darcie—"

"I'm not denying our baby. But Heather's got to be our first concern. We have to find the right time and way to tell her. We have to make sure she's okay with it."

He pulled her to him, tucked her face into his neck and rocked her. She could feel the tension in his arms, hear his heart beat beneath her ear. He was so warm, so familiar, her every fantasy. She'd loved him for so many years; she couldn't remember a time without him in her thoughts. And though she'd fantasized about having his arms around her like this, she hadn't really allowed herself to believe it could actually come to pass—aside from that one night five months ago.

But had she trapped him? Would he be holding her like this if it weren't for the baby growing in her womb? She'd given him the perfect opportunity to declare undying love for her. He hadn't taken the opportunity.

Frankly, she appreciated that about him, appreciated his honesty, that he hadn't lied just to placate her, to save her feelings.

Hope grew in her chest, though. He wanted her;

she could feel it in the arousal of his body pressed against hers. He held her so gently, his stroke so caring. He was a man who would protect, take care, nurture…excite.

And Heather seemed to like her. Maybe there was a chance…

She pulled back and stopped the thoughts before they got totally out of hand.

"I should get those kitty supplies out of my car."

"Can you stay for dinner? I'm trying my hand at crepes tonight."

"I need to get back to work." Her Ms. Fix-it antenna *did* raise a notch or two, though. Crepes were tricky and she'd bet money that he'd mess it up. Maybe he'd need some help.…

"It's late. Does the office still expect you back?"

"No, but I have a few accounts to call on still. I just sort of sandwiched the kitty delivery in between appointments."

"So come back when you're done. Let me impress you with my culinary skills."

She couldn't prevent the skeptical laughter that escaped.

"Hey, I heard that. Now that you've crushed my sensitive feelings, you're even more indebted. Besides, somebody's got to help me baby-sit the new kitty."

"The kitten's Heather's responsibility, Flynn. I'll give her the supplies and bring her up to speed on what needs to be done, but you should let her take charge of the care."

"True. But you didn't ask if the critter was convenient.'' He said it without accusation. ''Heather's going to a slumber party tonight. That leaves two babies—Mary Beth and the kitten—and me. Have pity.''

''You are such a conniver.'' She grinned, pulled open the door and headed for her car. He was right beside her.

''Around you a man's got to have a streak of con artist in him. You don't fall in with the plans when we want you to.''

She opened the trunk of her Honda and took out a bag of kitty litter and all manner of kitty supplies and toys. ''Those plans sound pretty suspicious to me.''

''I haven't got a nefarious bone in my body.'' Hefting the sack in one hand, he held up his fingers like an oath. ''Scouts' honor.''

''Shame on you.'' She knew playful insincerity when she saw it.

His brows rose. ''Chicken?'' he taunted softly.

''Don't pull that dare thing on me again, Flynn O'Grady.'' It was a point of honor that a Moretti not miss a dare.

''Aha. I've got your number now. Come to dinner. I dare you.''

''If you're lucky,'' she said, evading.

He caught her around the waist and pulled her to him, letting the bag drop to his feet. Before she even knew what he intended, his lips were on hers, taking, giving, caressing. She melted right into him, opened her mouth, circled his neck with her arms and pressed against him.

The winter air was crisp with the smell of pitch pine trees. A light, frigid breeze blew strands of her hair, tickling her cheeks.

It took several seconds for her to come to her senses.

She pulled back, sucked in a breath. "What in the world has gotten into you?"

"You," he said softly.

Oh, he knew how to knock a girl's heart askew. "We're out in the open. Anybody could see us."

"Nobody's watching, Darcie. I'm five acres away from my nearest neighbor."

"But Heather…" She glanced up at the leaded glass dormer windows.

"Heather's room is on the other side of the house."

"Well, I'm not coming to dinner if you plan to repeat this behavior."

"Chicken," he taunted again.

"I'm not chicken. I'm being sensible."

"You've got a responsibility to the kitty," he reminded. "I've never owned any pets—besides a dog when I was a kid. I don't know the first thing about taking care of a cat. You've got to give instructions."

"You're not playing fair."

"I never said I would."

Darcie ought to have her head examined for even considering coming back when she knew that they would be essentially alone.

Her reaction to that kiss was warning enough that

she wouldn't be able to resist Flynn if he put his mind to seduction.

And at a weak moment, what if he talked her into saying yes to his proposal? She couldn't let that happen, no matter how much she wanted to be part of his life, no matter how much she wanted a full-time father for their child.

But she could come for dinner—to supervise the crepes and check on the kitty.

Nothing said she had to stay past the time that Heather left.

THE CREPES WEREN'T half bad and Flynn was showing off like a typical male who considered himself a "can-do" guy.

Darcie laughed and swatted him with a dish towel. "Don't get too cocky. There's still tomorrow's dinner, and the day after that, and the day after that...."

"Killjoy," he said. "Can't you let me bask in my success?"

Heather walked in carrying the kitten and a duffel bag for her overnight stay at her girlfriend's house. She rolled her eyes at her father's boasting. "He does this strutting thing a lot. I even saw him dancing with the mop the other day."

His cheeks actually turned red. Darcie was charmed.

"You're a disrespectful, ungrateful kid," he said fondly.

"But you love me anyway." Heather said the words easily, but for some reason they seemed to give her a twinge. The sparkle of humor dimmed in her eyes.

Darcie wondered if this had been some sort or ritual between her and her mother and father.

Suddenly she felt out of place. She turned and wiped at the countertop.

"You're going to spoil that kitten by carrying it everywhere. Why don't you put her in her basket?"

"No. I'm taking her to Sabrina's house."

"I don't think—"

"But, Dad. I can't leave her alone."

"I'm home. And, besides, did you clear it with Sabrina's mother?"

"Of course. But like she'd care." Heather's eyes rolled so far back in her head, it was a wonder she didn't fall over. "Mrs. Leonard totally loves animals."

"Still, maybe I should talk to her, make sure—"

Heather's expression turned mutinous. "I can't believe you don't trust me!"

Darcie figured she ought to intervene before the innocent conversation turned into a war. "Sweetie, he does trust you." She stepped between father and daughter. "It's purely a courtesy thing that he talk to Sabrina's mom. You wouldn't want her to assume that your dad didn't care, would you? She might think that he was foisting an animal off on her, and taking for granted that she was okay with it."

"She's not like that."

"I'm sure she's not, but you never know. She might *think* it. Don't you ever think stuff, but keep it to yourself?"

"I guess." Heather looked at Flynn. "Sorry, Daddy."

Funny, how when she was contrite or scared, she called him "Daddy." When she was upset, she called him "Dad."

The doorbell rang. "That's them!" She hurriedly kissed Flynn on the cheek. "Bye, Darcie." She charged out of the room.

Flynn adopted his daughter's gesture and rolled his eyes. "I'll be right back," he said to Darcie, and went to the front door to speak with Mrs. Leonard.

Darcie folded the dish towel, then unfolded it, placing it on the countertop to dry. She heard the front door close and her heart sped up.

Mary Beth was already in bed.

With Heather gone, they were basically alone in the house.

Lord, she needed to get out of here.

She'd stalled too long, though, because when she looked up, Flynn stood in the doorway, watching her like a starving man might gaze upon a lavish banquet.

"Um...I should be going."

He pushed away from the doorjamb, came across the room, slowly, never taking his eyes from hers, masculine intent in his measured stride.

Her entire body trembled in anticipation. For a split second, she felt as though she might faint. Something weird was taking place inside her, something that she didn't know how to control.

And Darcie hated to be out of control.

But she was transfixed, caught in a way that she

knew would haunt her for a long time to come, held in a mesmerizing spell she was helpless to break.

He stopped in front of her, slid his hand lightly along her jaw and tunneled his fingers in her hair. The heat of his palm nearly scorched her.

"Stay," he said softly, and lowered his lips to hers.

Chapter Eight

Darcie couldn't resist. He drew her in, fitted her hips to his and pressed. Her heartbeat went wild, as did her imagination. She knew this man's touch, craved it. He made her ache, and he made her want to cry.

Reverently, gently, he angled his head and hers, taking the kiss higher, harder, pulling her closer. She tasted coffee and desire on his tongue, felt the unbreakable, unexplainable electricity in his touch. The chemistry between them was like an unstoppable wildfire, coursing through her, jumping to him and back again. A tangible, licking flame that could burn them if they weren't careful.

She tried to insert a sensible word, but barely got it out. "We—"

"We should," he murmured against her lips, somehow knowing her protest and determined to overcome it.

And Darcie didn't have a lot of argument in her. How could her mind go blank when so many impressions were crowding in? Words flashed through her brain, but none stuck long enough for her to consider them, or remember them. She could only feel. The caress of Flynn's fingers. The strength of his body.

And she could only yearn. For something she wanted more than life, but knew she very likely couldn't have.

Oh, the ache was enough to send her to her knees. But Flynn's strong arms were around her, holding her, making her feel as though things had a prayer of working out.

"Come upstairs with me," he said, his voice rough. "I did you wrong the last time. I was rushed and had too much to drink. This time I want to make it last, do it right, show you that I'm not an insensitive jerk."

"I know…I know you're not."

"Let me prove it anyway."

His lips cruised to her ear, her neck. She shivered at the erotic sensations that coursed through her.

"We can't."

"I want to see your tattoo."

She made herself step back. "I'll show it to you…but we don't have to go that far just to see it."

He let her go, didn't even try to disguise the aroused state of his body straining at the front of his jeans. "You're gonna drop your drawers and expect me to keep my hands in my pockets?"

"A gentleman would."

"Did I say I was a gentleman?" She'd moved just a bit farther away from him, he noted.

"You don't have to say it, Flynn. I can see it."

"Then I'm definitely slipping. Used to be I had a bad-boy image that made women shiver just to look at."

She put him right in his place when she burst out laughing. Just as he'd intended for her to do. She was looking way too serious, way too scared—as though she would leave and never return. He wanted to persuade her otherwise. But he knew when to back off and when to press. Right now was the time for backing off.

"Nothing wrong with your ego," she said.

"Look closer, darlin'. You've just stomped on it."

She shook her head. "I really have to go."

"Why? It's Friday night. Got a pressing date?"

"Maybe."

He felt his gut tighten. "If it's not with me, then cancel it."

"I can see how your daughter might object to your bossiness."

"I'm not bossy."

She raised her brows.

He let out a breath. "I want to spend time with you, Darcie." His voice softened. "I want to make love with you." He never looked away. "I want you to marry me."

For no reason whatsoever, tears flooded her eyes. He looked horrified.

"Hey! What's wrong?" He was at her side in an instant.

She waved him away. "Nothing. This happens all

the time lately and I don't seem to have any control.''

Softly, reverently, he placed his palm over her stomach. ''The baby?''

That caused the tears to spill over. ''I wish things were different, Flynn, but they aren't. You're not in love with me.'' When he started to speak, she blazed ahead. ''And even if you were, you can't control your daughter's emotions. I have more experience in this area than you do. I've spent more than ten years listening to troubled or sad teens who've called the runaway hot line. I know how they think. And I know that just because we adults will it, that doesn't mean they'll come around to our way of thinking.''

''Heather's a loving girl at heart. If we give her time—''

''Maybe. But we're not going to push this, Flynn. I won't push her. I won't sacrifice her for my own feelings.''

He pounced on that. ''And what are your feelings, Darcie?''

She could have lied. But that didn't feel right. So she simply evaded. ''What do you think?'' If he were as smart as he looked, he'd figure it out.

She picked up her coat off the back of the kitchen chair and slipped it on. Passing him, she lightly kissed his cheek.

Big mistake. He took the opportunity to draw her close, to hold her, to turn his head, take her lips and deepen the kiss. After several minutes of mind-boggling sensation, he let her go, holding on to her arms only long enough to make sure she was steady.

She didn't think she'd ever be steady again in her life.

"That's a powerful thing between us, Darcie Moretti. Don't deny it."

"I'm not denying it, Flynn." Interesting how he turned it back to desire rather than press her on her feelings. Maybe he really didn't realize how she felt. Was it only that she felt it so strongly that she assumed he would understand? Pick up on it? And why in the world did she want him to so badly? At this particular time in their lives, it was hopeless. "I'm only saying it can't go any further."

"For God's sake, it's already gone further. You're having my baby."

"Women have babies by themselves all the time."

"But *you* don't have to!"

"Haven't you been listening to me?"

"Of course I have. You're pregnant with my child. I've asked you to marry me. You've practically said you love me!"

"But you don't love me back!" They were shouting at each other right there in the kitchen, each breathing hard.

"How do you know?"

"Because… Oh, never mind!" She wanted to pull out her hair, wanted to just sit down in the middle of the ivory tile floor and howl. Life was so damned unfair. "The fact that your daughter is still calling the hot line is a prime reason that we should not be having this conversation.''

''She—'' He swore. ''Why didn't you tell me?''

''The hot line is confidential.''

''We're past that, Darcie. If you married me, she wouldn't have to call. You'd be right here for her to talk to.''

''And what if that backfired?''

''I believe she'll come to accept it.''

''I'm not willing to take that chance and you shouldn't be, either.''

''Fine. Then just be our friend for now. Is that too much to ask?''

Put like that, it shamed her to say yes, that it was *indeed* too much to ask. Because to give in, to continue to remain this close to him, to his girls, to allow the dream to take hold, would be setting herself up for heartache. And she wasn't a masochist by any stretch of the imagination.

''Please,'' he said softly, his eyes filled with need and something else she couldn't define.

Oh, hell's bells, she thought. Ms. Softie's fix-it antenna was shooting up again.

''You and I don't do friendship very well, Flynn.''

His sexy lips curved and she regretted her words. They did other things very well. That was the unspoken message between them.

Then he sobered and stepped close, his eyes serious. He tipped up her chin, made her meet his gaze. ''Our lives are entwined whether you like it or not—whether Heather likes it or not. Give us a chance to see how things go, okay? You can't just walk out on us.''

She wished she had a crystal ball, or the gift of second sight. She wanted to know it would all work out okay. She wanted to believe that the dream could come true, that *her* dream could come true. She'd fallen so hard for this man—and for his children. She wanted badly for them to be a unit.

''Give us a chance, Darcie. We'll take it slow. Let Heather warm up to us.''

She couldn't say no. Because this was her dream. ''Okay. We'll take it slow. But Heather's going to be our barometer, Flynn. It can't be any other way.''

He nodded, although a sadness dimmed his eyes. They both knew that they couldn't sacrifice one of his daughters for another.

THE DAY HAD GONE to hell in a hurry. And it was barely ten o'clock in the morning. With one arm around her neighbor Mr. Bentley and the other cradling Hollingsworth, her old Persian cat, Darcie stood outside her apartment building, shock making her numb. She wouldn't even have been here, but she'd ripped a hole in her tights getting into her car, and being close to home, thought to run back real quick and grab another pair.

That's when she'd seen the flames.

And the fire engines.

Oh, dear God, what next? The very fabric of her life seemed to be fraying lately, little by little, events happening that she had no control over. And the threads just kept breaking, snags that she couldn't fix.

Irrationally she felt like laughing when she glanced at Mr. Bentley. His gray hair stuck up at odd angles and his fire-engine-red sleep shirt hung sadly off his bony shoulders.

But this was no laughing matter. The Trenton fire department was very real, its firefighters in full protective gear pumping water on the burning structure in front of her. The building was a total loss.

And all Darcie's worldly possessions were gone with it.

On the heels of hysterical laughter, came a sense of surreal stillness, emptiness and then heart-pounding adrenaline that made her want to run and hide, to pretend that this wasn't happening.

But she was a practical woman. And her stinging eyes and the acrid stench of billowing smoke told her it was indeed reality.

Her life had just gone up in flames—never mind that her furniture was all mismatched and that her pregnancy ensured that she didn't fit into any of her clothes. They were her clothes and her furniture. Her sense of independence.

Her security for her unborn child.

Tears dripped off her cheeks onto Hollingsworth's fur. The old Persian cat looked up at her, docile for once. Normally he considered himself too good to be held. Obviously he understood that this was a bad day to act up.

She felt Mr. Bentley's arm tighten around her

waist and she looked at him. "Are you all right?" she asked.

"No, but what can we do?"

"You're right. Do you have someplace to go?"

"Yes. My daughter's on her way. I've got plenty of money in savings to get another place, so I won't have to impose on her long...." He took a breath. "Listen to me, talking as though this is no big deal."

"I understand," she said softly. People reacted weirdly in disasters. It would hit them all later. "The important thing is that we all got out, that no one was hurt. Do you have any idea how the fire started?"

"I expect the fire department will take a while in its investigation, but if you ask me, I'm betting it was Lem Sniedmiller and those cigars he's always puffing on. Damned fool falls asleep at the drop of a pin, and half the time he's got a stogie between his fingers."

"Now, Mr. Bentley, we don't know this for sure and we shouldn't be tossing out accusations."

He looked at her, his liquid eyes still sharp and clear at eighty. A retired CPA, he'd been a wonderful adviser to her over the past six months that she'd lived in the apartment. "You're a good girl, Darcie. Sweet. Don't mind an old grouch like me."

She hugged him, and the action was too much for Hollingsworth, who leaped from her arms and glared at them for squishing him. His tail swished, but he didn't move too far from her, a dead giveaway that he wasn't as sure of himself as he wanted to act.

She would have troubles getting him in the car, though; he hated the car.

"How about you, missy? Do you have somewhere to go? Will you go home?"

The very thought made her itch as though she'd broken out in hives. She loved her family dearly, but she didn't want to live with them again. Plus, now that Grandma Connor had moved in, there wasn't room. And one bathroom between four adults wasn't Darcie's idea of a picnic. Especially with the way her bladder acted now that she was pregnant.

"I'm not sure, Mr. Bentley." She thought of Flynn, of the beautiful house in Princeton, of the huge beveled mirror over the fireplace, of how she'd felt like Cinderella when she'd descended the staircase.

But Flynn's home wasn't her castle. He wasn't her prince, no matter how much she wished it. And even if the glass slipper fit, the potential consequences of accepting the shoe were too enormous.

Nothing was certain in this life.

She'd just found that out in the worst possible way—staring at her home burning in front of her.

She turned when a car squealed to a stop in the parking lot.

"Ah, Millicent's here," Mr. Bentley said. "She's always been a prompt girl. Are you sure you'll be all right? You can come with us."

Darcie kissed Mr. Bentley on the cheek. "Thank you, but I'm fine. I've got my computer and my business papers here in the car. Plus I have an 'in' with the insurance people." She smiled. "I'll probably stay with my folks for a few days, but this isn't such a disaster for me. I'd planned to move anyway before the baby came. You go on with Millie and don't worry about me. I'll hang around a bit and talk to the firemen, see when we can come back and go through the building.''

"Don't hold out much hope that anything will be left.''

Millicent rushed up, putting her arm around her father, then lightly squeezing Darcie's hand, her eyes filled with fear and relief and compassion.

Darcie's heart nearly broke for Mr. Bentley. He'd lived in this building for thirty years, the last six he'd been alone since his beloved Alice had died. The loss for him was so much greater, the memories that had gone up in flames, the pictures, keepsakes, the remembrances of a lifetime that could never be replaced by insurance money.

Having only been here for six months, Darcie hadn't amassed a huge amount of irreplaceable treasures. Some, of course, but not nearly the magnitude that Mr. Bentley had.

A raindrop landed on her head, then another. Her breath blew white in the midmorning air. The sky was gunmetal gray, as though the nasty cloud of smoke had leached its disastrous tentacles over the whole city. The rain picked up and thunder rumbled off in the distance.

Hollingsworth bumped up against her leg, his wet fur tickling her through the wide run that was getting worse with each move she made. She reached down and picked up the cat.

"Don't act like such a tough guy," she said when he squirmed. She spread her coat and tried to wrap him up to keep him dry. "You're cold and wet just like I am and we're both getting in the car. No arguments."

She juggled the cat and the door, managed to make it into the cold, but dry interior of the car. Hollingsworth shot out of her arms and leaped into the back seat.

"Don't look at me that way," she said. "Just wait till we get to Mom and Dad's. You haven't met Grandma Connor, and you're in for a shock. But don't comment on the orange hair. And steer clear if she's got a gun...."

The ridiculous running conversation with the cat wasn't distracting enough. Darcie laid her head on the steering wheel, felt the tears slip down her cheeks. She didn't want to go home to her parents.

It felt wrong somehow, like she'd failed. They hadn't given her a hard time about being pregnant, but she felt guilty nonetheless. As long as she was living on her own, taking care of herself, it was okay. She could pretend that they weren't disappointed in her, that this was how everyone conducted their lives, that women had babies out of wedlock all the time and nobody thought a thing about it.

If she went home, it put her back to being the child and them the adults. It made it a whole new ball game.

It made her feel like a failure.

Her cell phone rang, scaring the daylights out of

her. Pressing a hand to her pumping heart, she took a breath, then reached for the flip phone. "Hello?"

"Hi…uh, it's Flynn."

Her heart pumped even harder. "I know." How could he think she wouldn't recognize his voice? She held her breath, her gaze focused on the apartment building that was still getting a water bath, both from the fire hoses and Mother Nature. Just the sound of Flynn's voice made her want to cry, and that was ridiculous. But there it was anyway. If she breathed, a sob would escape. She was sure of it. And she was feeling too raw to show many more vulnerabilities.

"It's a good sign when you recognize my voice. Means we're making progress. I called to invite you to dinner. And before you say no, I should tell you this kitten that you brought over is acting like a wild thing. You've got to come and see for yourself, give us some pointers."

She tried to clear her throat, held her palm over the mouthpiece of the phone, widened her eyelids to keep the tears from spilling over.

"Darcie? Are you still there?"

"Mmm."

A pause. "What's wrong? Where are you?"

She took another breath, sniffed, realized that the sob would not escape after all. She was tough, just like she'd told Hollingsworth to be. She'd beat it back. "I'm sitting in my car in front of my apartment building."

"Why…? Darcie, are you crying?"

Her eyeballs felt strained so she simply closed them. "Did I mention that the building's burning?"

Two beats of dead silence. Then, "My God, are you all right? Do you want me to come get you? Of course I should come get you. Stay put. I'll—"

"No! Flynn, I'm fine."

"You are not. You're shaken up. I can hear it. You're *crying.*" It almost sounded like an accusation. She nearly smiled. "You shouldn't drive."

"I'm a Moretti. I can drive."

"Tough girl."

"Yep, that's me. I will take you up on the dinner invite, though. Seems I'm a little short on stoves and groceries at the moment."

"Ah, sweetheart, I'm sorry."

That brought fresh tears to sting her eyes and clog her throat. She wished that the coast was clear for her to truly be his sweetheart. "Yeah, me, too."

EVER PRACTICAL, Darcie stopped by the mall on her way to Flynn's house. All she needed were a few essentials, she told herself. But her list kept growing. She tried to go at it from a light attitude, pretending she was packing for a weekend trip.

After the first forty-five minutes, her nerves were totally frayed.

And her bank account was scraping rock bottom, not to mention the decibels at which her credit cards were screaming.

But she prided herself on keeping it together, on smiling, on finishing up the day at work and putting in a couple of hours at the hot line. There were plenty of other people—teens to be exact—who were much worse off than she was. Teens who were sleeping on the streets on a night when the temperatures were expected to drop below freezing.

At least Darcie knew she was welcome at her parent's house—although there were no spare rooms. She'd slept on the couch before in a pinch, and she could do so again.

But she wouldn't. She would look in Flynn's Yellow Pages in a few minutes and pick out a motel that had a kitchenette and rented by the week. Then she'd concentrate on finding a new apartment or a small house like she'd wanted to before....

Before her apartment had burned, along with her clothes and furniture—before she'd drained her bank account and put a big ding in her credit cards.

Now she sat on Flynn's sofa, staring at the fire in the fireplace. The meat loaf had been a bit charred, but it had filled the hollow ache in her stomach. The mashed potatoes out of the box were too easy to screw up. The dessert, on the other hand, wouldn't win any Martha Stewart awards. Darcie had given it a pass. She didn't need the extra calories anyway. Sugar was bad for the baby.

Her gaze landed on a family photo album on the coffee table. And out of nowhere, the strength she'd pretended to possess crumbled, and tears welled up and spilled over her lashes.

Even though she hadn't lived in the apartment long, she *had* lost some things that were precious and irreplaceable. Family photographs, her high school yearbook and the secret mementos she'd kept of Flynn—his picture in the paper alongside a write-up of his architect award, her journals where she'd recorded her feelings. Not that she'd want to look at them again, or for anybody to see them. But they were her *things*. She would miss them.

And to have to start over was doubly devastating with the baby coming. She felt so inadequate and overwhelmed.

Flynn saw the devastation on Darcie's face the minute he and Heather walked into the room after finishing the dishes. He put Mary Beth in the play-pen with her toys to occupy her, then went directly to Darcie, pulling her to him on the couch, rubbing her back, trying to soothe, but terribly afraid he was doing a bad job of it.

"Shh, it'll be okay."

"Dad," Heather said, sitting down next to them on the couch, baby kitty in her arms. "Her house burned. It's *not* okay."

"So, fine, I'm an insensitive dork. I don't know what else to say."

Darcie smiled and reached out to squeeze Heather's hand. "It's okay, Heather. I understand and appreciate his concern. And yours, too."

Flynn's arms tightened for just an instant. That she could offer comfort or run interference in the midst of her misery proved she was always thinking of others.

Then again, did he really need proof of that? Her incessant thinking about others was the main reason she wouldn't marry him.

He didn't want to feel good about this latest

disaster, but he couldn't help but hope it was a point for his side. If Darcie didn't have a home to go to, perhaps she'd finally give in and agree to his suggestion that she move in with them, a suggestion he'd been bringing up at five-minute intervals ever since she'd arrived.

And at each interval she'd shushed him, put him off, her gaze darting to Heather.

Hell, they weren't doing anything wrong. Heather was going to have to learn about the baby soon. But Darcie wasn't ready. And with her life in upheaval like this, he didn't feel right about pushing.

Getting her to move in with them, though, was another matter entirely.

He would play by fair means or foul.

He glanced at his daughter, at the compassion she clearly felt for Darcie, and realized that she didn't appear belligerent that he was holding Darcie in his arms, comforting her. Heather seemed to accept it, almost acting like he wasn't doing nearly enough. Then again, she didn't know the history between him and Darcie.

"I'm sorry," Darcie said, sitting up, pulling away from Flynn. "I don't mean to fall apart this way. It's silly."

It was a subtle withdrawal, but Flynn understood the reason. She didn't want Heather to get any ideas or come to any correct conclusions. At least not yet. Not like this.

"There's nothing silly about it, Darc. You're human."

"Yeah, well this human's got to make some plans and find a room at the inn."

"You could stay with us," Heather said. "Isn't that right, Daddy? We've got tons of rooms that aren't being used."

"No, really, honey—" Darcie started.

"That's a great idea," Flynn said, pouncing, acting as though it were totally Heather's idea, that he hadn't been hounding her about the same thing all night. "It makes good sense. There's not a lot of room at your folks' house."

She gave him a look.

"Well, I've been there. Do you really want to wake up to Grandma Connor every morning?"

Heather was horrified, and gave another censorious "Dad."

Darcie's laugh ended on a hiccup. "Shame on you, Flynn."

"I've seen your grandma, too. And she's a great old lady, but you don't want to live with her."

"I didn't say I was going to live with her. I'm going to a motel."

"Don't be so damned stubborn."

"Mr. Charm," Darcie muttered, her gaze snagging on his. His chocolate eyes were determined and hot. It gave her a thrill. Then she remembered that Heather was sitting on the couch with them, and she cleared her throat, stood and went to Mary Beth's playpen. The baby held up her little arms and Darcie picked her up, nuzzling her soft cheek.

"Did you or did you not put a hell of a strain on your finances to replace the essentials today?"

"Yes, but—"

"Then you should be wanting to save money at every turn. We've got the room here. And it's free."

"No way. If I stay here, I'm paying rent."

"Fine. A dollar a day."

"Ten."

"Fifty cents."

"Okay, eight."

"Ten cents. Deal's closed."

"Cool!" Heather said. "You can have the yellow room. It's all fixed up. And you can watch baby kitty grow."

"Baby kitty's not going to grow much bigger if she doesn't learn to sleep at night," Flynn said.

"Don't say stuff like that. She'll hear you." Heather hugged the kitten and turned slightly away from her father as though he would actually follow through with his veiled threat. Darcie was still trying to figure out how she'd gotten palatial living quarters for a dime a day. It sounded like a telephone company ad.

"Well, I hear her plenty in the dead of night," Flynn continued to his daughter. "That kitten's all over the place, bouncing off the walls, using the staircase as a raceway. Twice I've expected to come down here and find a prowler ransacking the place, the way she gets into everything."

"You're just mad about her spilling the juice on your blueprints."

"Damn cat knocked over a glass I'd left out," Flynn explained to Darcie.

"Serves you right for leaving it out," Heather admonished.

Flynn made a playful swipe at his daughter. "Respect your elders, kiddo."

She giggled. "So are you staying, Darcie?"

It was such a big decision. Staying in close quarters with this family would be both joy and anguish. It would cause her hopes to soar, and it would be a constant reminder of what she couldn't have.

What she couldn't allow herself to have.

Heather was innocently agreeing to a boarder, a friend who'd brought them a kitten, who'd talked to her on the other end of a runaway hot line. She didn't know that there was intimacy going on between Darcie and her Dad. She didn't know that Darcie was carrying a baby in her womb who was Heather's half sister.

She didn't know that Flynn was determined to make Darcie a permanent part of the family. A dreaded stepmom.

Just like Tammy's father had done.

What then?

But tonight, right now, Darcie was exhausted, and vulnerable. She needed to believe in something, in someone, needed to be part of this family, to dream.

She swallowed the lump in her throat, stroked Mary Beth's temples, noting that the baby's eyes had drifted closed. "Yes, I'd like to stay for a few days. At least until I can find a new place."

Hollingsworth, who'd been hiding behind a potted rubber tree, peeked his head out at that, glared at all the adults and arched his back at the sight of the mischievous baby kitty, then gave Darcie a green-eyed stare that seemed to radiate accusation and warning.

But as much as Darcie knew she should heed that warning, she just couldn't.

She wanted to be close to Flynn. She wanted to be part of this family. For both herself and her baby.

Chapter Nine

Darcie kept herself busy over the next few days. She was constantly on the Internet checking her stock figures. She hooked up her modem to Flynn's fax line so she wouldn't cramp his or Heather's style.

Determined to pull her weight, to pay for her lodging, she tackled the mountain of dirty laundry that had piled up on the O'Grady's service porch, and rearranged the pantry shelves in between making phone calls to her clients.

And although it was getting harder to find excuses, she tried to stay away every night.

She couldn't let herself be alone with Flynn. The chemistry between them was like an inferno. And she was getting worn down. Perhaps she'd go to the yoga class tonight. Maybe Elaine Steadwell would want to go, too. Then she decided against calling her friend. Elaine and Ross were newlyweds.

And Darcie didn't need to think about newlyweds and what they did.

She was having enough trouble keeping her wayward emotions under control as it was.

It was ridiculous how Flynn walked around the house practically naked. He had *girls* in residence, for heaven's sake! Heather and Mary Beth shouldn't be treated to the sight of him in pajama bottoms and no shirt! Perfectly decent, of course, but still too sexy. Too sexy for Darcie's peace of mind.

She gathered up her papers, made a few more notes about the mutual fund she'd recommended Ula Mae invest in, then shut off her computer.

Without the whir of the hard drive, the room seemed unnaturally silent. With its yellow walls and ivory candlewicking bedspread, it was a restful room.

But Darcie wasn't feeling restful.

She felt rest*less*.

A sound at the doorway made her head whip up. Flynn stood with his shoulder against the jamb, his chocolate eyes flaring with the desire she'd come to recognize every time he looked at her. It was thrilling, made her insides ache, made her heart flutter and her mind take off on flights of fancy.

Fanciful dreams of family and love and togetherness. Togetherness in bed.

She cleared her throat, looked away, fussed with the laptop.

"Finished for the day?" he asked.

"For a while, at least." She didn't want to admit that she was at loose ends. Then she'd have no excuse to avoid him, no defenses. And that was very dangerous. Especially with the way her hormones were acting.

"You've been avoiding me." He pushed away from the wall and came into the room.

She swore she could feel his warmth, although he was still several feet from her. It radiated from him.

Oh, she was being so silly.

"I've been busy," she said evasively.

"You're a terrible liar, Darc." He was at the foot of the bed now, his knee bumping against hers. She couldn't even stand in order to get away because that would bring the front of her body right up against his.

"Are you suggesting I'm not pulling my weight around here?"

He shook his head, raised a brow at the stack of neatly folded clothes on her bed—mostly his socks and Mary Beth's sleepers. "You're reaching."

"And you're crowding me."

"I'd like to do a lot more than that."

"Flynn," she warned.

"Don't 'Flynn' me. I know you feel what's going on between us."

"The kids are in the house."

"Heather rode her bike to a friend's house. She won't be back until suppertime. And Mary Beth's napping." He stopped for a moment, frowned. "Although she probably shouldn't be sleeping this late in the afternoon. She'll be up all night."

"She'll be fine. She's probably going through a growing spurt."

"Think so?"

"I'm no expert, but it makes sense."

He reached down, surprising her, and hooked his

hands gently around her upper arms, bringing her up to stand with her chest against his. Her heart throbbed, and so did everything else within her. He smelled of blueprint ink and fabric softener. "Marry me, Darcie."

She pulled away from him, though it was one of the hardest things she'd ever done. "Don't start with me, Flynn."

"Why not? We need to talk about us."

She shook her head.

He tucked his finger under her chin, stopped the movement and made her look at him. "Yes. We need to talk about that night, what happened and why."

"What's to talk about? It was sex, pure and simple." This time she successfully evaded him by stepping away. She didn't want to go down this conversational path with him. It was risky. No sense burdening him with her feelings that she'd had since she was a girl.

He didn't return those feelings. And it would put him in an awkward position to admit that. Especially since he was so hell-bent on getting her to marry him.

And getting her back into bed.

"I think it was more than that."

"Okay, you're right. Alcohol was involved."

He winced. "I've apologized for that." Breaching her defenses again, he stepped up to her, ran a finger over the shoulder of her sweatshirt, leaving a trail of fire beneath. "And I've offered to make it right."

"That's exactly how we could get ourselves in big trouble."

He grinned—a little sadly, it seemed. "I already got you in trouble."

She felt her face heat. Knowing it and having it said out loud were two different things. She wasn't a prude by any means, but sometimes she felt shy around him.

And she felt needy.

And she really wanted him. Bad.

His thumb moved up her neck, stroking, then to her bottom lip, his gaze following. "I want you, Darcie."

"I know," she whispered. "But we can't always have what we want."

"Bet me." His lips closed over hers, stealing any protest she might have made. His palms scorched her through the material of the sweatshirt. With a sure touch, he drew her to him, settled her firmly in the nest of his hips and sent her fantasies skyrocketing. He was aroused, and she could feel him pressed against the juncture of her thighs. She pushed closer, trying to climb up his body, forgetting every reason why they shouldn't be doing this.

Her hands were feverish with need and they swept over him, touching where she could. Angling her head for a deeper kiss, she begged without uttering a sound.

Her breath sounded loud in her ears; her blood pumped wildly through her veins.

Mary Beth cried.

Darcie pulled away.

Flynn raked a hand through his hair, knew he'd lost her, that her objections were firmly back in place. His frustration was like a volcano about to spew hot lava. Everything inside him felt as though it were churning, boiling. Part of it was sexual, he knew that. But the biggest part was helplessness. He couldn't *make* Darcie see things his way, couldn't *make* her tell him stuff, or share herself with him, or go to bed with him, or marry him.

He wasn't the swiftest guy on the block when it came to running a household, and God knows he was making plenty of costly mistakes—the washer repair bill was a prime example. But at least he was trying.

That was more than he felt he was getting from Darcie. He wanted to tell her this, but Mary Beth's wails were getting louder.

"We're not through with this, Darcie."

Darcie read his sensually loaded threat loud and clear. Oh, his words hadn't given him away. It was the look in his eyes, the way they'd dropped to her mouth, then lower. Darcie figured she'd best hit the streets in search of other living arrangements very soon.

And she would. Just as soon as her checking account showed a positive balance, a balance that would cover a first and last month's deposit.

She nearly groaned. That could take a while.

And just as she'd feared, her resolve was crumbling fast where Flynn O'Grady was concerned. If they hadn't been interrupted by the baby, she'd have given in to his sensual demands…and made several of her own to boot.

FLYNN DONNED AN APRON and put a plate on top of the cookbook to keep it open. Problem was, then he couldn't see the directions. He removed the plate and the book closed.

"How the hell do people do this?"

"Problems?" Darcie asked, standing just inside the kitchen doorway, briefcase in her hand. He knew her laptop computer was in that case, and that meant she was about to either leave the house or hole up in her room hooked up to the Internet.

He didn't want her to leave. He wanted her company.

"Not big ones. Just trying to figure out how to keep the book open."

She moved forward, pulled a wire stand from behind the cookie jar and set the book on it. Slick as oil, it held the book open and at the perfect angle to read.

"I wondered what that thing was for. I nearly threw it out." He ran a fingertip over her cheek, her lips, deliberately trying to arouse. He was successful, too, if the flare in her hazel eyes was any indication. "You're handy to have around."

"Yep, that's me. Handy Darcie."

"I meant that in the best way."

"That's what all the guys say," she said flippantly, attempting to step back.

He stopped her. "From now on, the only guy who better be saying stuff to you is me."

"You're not exactly in a position to make those kind of demands."

He held on to his temper. Patience wasn't one of his strong suits, but he was learning. It was sort of a baptism by fire lately. Between Heather and Mary Beth and that wild kitten, and now Darcie's stubbornness, he deserved to be nominated for sainthood. "I am *too* in a position. And I'm going to get you there, too." He lowered his voice, held her gaze so she would be sure exactly what he was talking about. "And one of those positions is going to be horizontal."

She sucked in a breath. "Flynn—"

"I know. Don't start. The kids will hear." He knew the drill. "You're going to get tired of running, Darcie Moretti. And I'm going to catch you."

She sat heavily in the chair and he grinned.

That earned him a glare, and he laughed. "You doubt me?"

"You'll catch me if I *want* you to."

"But you do," he said softly, then turned back to his recipe, smiling to himself when he heard her exhale.

He knew when to retreat. And her reaction gave him confidence that he hadn't forgotten all his seductive techniques.

He'd just decided exactly how he'd handle her when he got her in bed. Advance and retreat—in the best possible way, of course. He would take her to the edge, then pull back, let her anticipate, then he would start again, stronger, higher, take her further.

The seduction of Darcie Moretti would be slow

and thorough. And when he was done, he'd do it again. And again. Until he'd convinced her that they belonged together...that they should be a family.

Heather came in the room carrying Mary Beth. That in itself made Flynn suspicious. She didn't normally get her sister up from a nap without putting up a fuss.

He glanced her way, then did a double-take, his eyes narrowing. The short skirt and skimpy sweater were more dressy than an evening at home warranted. It bugged him when she got all ready to go someplace before she'd even asked if she could go.

"What're you cooking?" she asked, her tone bouncy and congenial. Too congenial.

He pointed to the package of chicken breasts thawing on the tile countertop. "I was looking for that recipe that Grandma does with the chilies and cheese."

She came over and flipped through the cookbook. "Here it is. Uh, I'm not that hungry, though, so you shouldn't plan on me."

Mary Beth leaned out of Heather's arms, reaching for Flynn. He took the baby. "What's up, kiddo?"

Heather sat down at the table, fussed with the salt shaker. "Liz wants me to stay the night at her house. And..."

Flynn interrupted her. "Wait a minute. I thought you and Liz weren't friends anymore."

"We've straightened that out. Anyway, daddy, you remember I'm on the committee for the Valentine's Day dance, right?" Her words came faster. "I told you last week that there was a meeting tonight to figure out the decorating. And it's good that Darcie's here. I won't feel bad leaving you, because she can help with Mary Beth. Won't you, Darcie?''

"Well..."

"See? She said yes."

Both Flynn and Darcie were struck speechless at that. Then Darcie chuckled. "You're a con artist, kiddo."

Heather grinned. "Yeah, but Daddy's looking like he's in a fog again. I *did* tell him about the dance."

"Maybe you did," Flynn said. "But for the benefit of my approaching senility, why don't you run it by me again?"

She rolled her eyes at his drama—as though she wasn't the drama queen herself, Flynn thought. And when the heck had she ever worried about leaving him alone with Mary Beth?

It took two explanations but he finally understood she was going to a dance at the high school to get decorating ideas for the Valentine's Day dance she and Liz were working on.

"Is Robbie Sanders going to be at this dance?" he couldn't help asking.

"Probably. But I'm not with him anymore."

"You're not?" Relief made him nearly sag against the counter. With that kind of news he'd consider giving her the keys to the car—never mind that she wouldn't have a license for three years yet.

"No. He's going out with some cheerleader."

"Two-timer." He wasn't sorry about the breakup. He never did trust that kid.

"By the way, how did you plan to get into a high school dance?"

"It's a special thing the school's doing. They want to start early with us eighth graders so that when we finally get there, we'll want to be involved."

He nodded. "What time is it over?"

"Nine-thirty. And that's like totally early for a Friday night. Plus, a parent has to sign us in and out, so you don't have to worry."

"Okay, I guess I could take you."

"No. Liz's mom's gonna do it."

"Are you embarrassed of me?" Flynn asked, his expression crestfallen.

"I'm not embarrassed of you, Daddy." Obviously seeing an opening and possible victory in sight, Heather had segued into sweet and reasonable mode. "But you've got to take care of Mary Beth. And you shouldn't leave Darcie here all by herself, either."

Darcie's heart leaped. Heather was giving permission for her to be alone with Flynn. Trouble was, the girl had no idea how volatile that could be. How volatile it had been once upon a time. Over five months ago to be exact.

"I don't need to be entertained."

"I know," Heather said. "But you probably could use somebody to hang out with, couldn't you?"

"Yeah, couldn't you?" Flynn echoed. He looked at Darcie, noticed the high color on her cheeks. He turned back to Heather. "Okay. You can go."

She leaped up, shrieked in glee, kissed him, then charged out of the room.

It was ridiculous how good he felt when she was happy like this. Still, he wouldn't shirk his parental responsibilities.

He'd talk to Liz's mother and make sure that everything was on the up and up.

Then he would enjoy the evening with Darcie.

Alone.

Exactly what he'd wanted to do.

He needed time to convince her that they belonged together as a family. And to do that would take some finesse, some thought...some seduction.

It would be best all around to have the house to themselves.

Chapter Ten

Mary Beth fell asleep against Darcie's shoulder. Darcie loved the warm feel of the baby against her chest, loved the sweet smell of her freshly washed hair. It seemed so natural to press her lips against the chubby cheek of the sleeping child.

Oh, she loved this baby as though she'd come from her own womb. And she loved Heather, too. They were easy children to love.

But that didn't mean they would love her back. The baby, yes, because she didn't have the memories and the wounds. But Heather was a pressure cooker. Handle her wrong and she could blow.

"Want me to take her?" Flynn asked. He'd done the dishes while she'd bathed and rocked Mary Beth.

"I can carry her." Darcie stood, a smile tugging at her mouth when Flynn hovered, his gaze shooting to her pregnant stomach. She liked his solicitous behavior toward her, but cautioned herself not to get too used to it.

Even though she wanted to in the worst possible way.

He followed her up the stairs. From the mirror over the fireplace, she could see their reflection as they ascended the stairs, could see the rapt, unguarded look on Flynn's face as he watched her.

She knew what was on his mind. Unbridled desire had been like a tangible thing between them since the moment Liz and her mother had picked up Heather.

She paused, allowing Flynn to go ahead of her into the nursery. He flicked on the teddy bear lamp and lowered the side of the crib, then stepped aside as Darcie eased Mary Beth to the mattress and covered her with a soft blanket.

Their fingers brushed as they both smoothed the fleece up to Mary Beth's chin. Darcie's eyes jerked to Flynn's.

She saw his gaze shift from her eyes to her stomach. The unspoken message was that they could be doing this together one of these days soon for their own baby.

She wanted that so bad she could taste it. And because it wasn't wise to want things she couldn't allow herself to have, she broke eye contact and moved out of the nursery, only making it as far as the hallway before he caught her arm, turned her and pulled her against him.

It was pitiful how it only took a mere look or touch from him to make her melt, to make her forget all about good intentions. To make her feel selfish, to want, to consider tossing every other concern or responsibility to the wind in order to experience him. Just once more.

"You know this isn't a good idea, Flynn."

"It's an excellent idea—the only one either of us can think about, and you know it."

She started to shake her head. He stopped the movement by pressing his lips against her jaw. "You're a terrible liar. Besides, we agreed to take it a day at a time. And so far, Heather isn't giving us any trouble."

An image of Tammy putting on a brave front flashed in Darcie's mind, but she dismissed it. She wanted Flynn. Wanted to take what he was offering. Tenderness. Intimacy. She longed to be close to him. To touch him. To have him touch her. To stoke the raging fire that had burned for them that night over five months ago.

Nobody had to know.

"Let me make love to you, Darcie. With the lights on this time and our eyes wide open and me cold sober." His fingertips caressed her cheek, skimmed her neck, her collarbone, and then slowly grazed the upper swell of her breasts.

She drew in a breath, couldn't seem to speak, then exhaled on a moan as his fingers worked a sensual assault over the tips of her breasts. Even through the barriers of her knit top and bra, the stimulation was intense.

"Say yes," he coaxed. For endless moments he simply held her with his gaze.

And Darcie came undone. "Yes."

"Yes!" he repeated, his voice a near exultant

shout. He bent, hooked her behind the knees and lifted her in his arms.

"Flynn—"

"Shh, baby, don't fight me."

"I'm not.... I can walk."

"And I can carry you."

Oh, could he ever. He could carry her to the moon and back. The heat in his eyes alone was enough to launch a rocket. She wanted him with a fierceness that stunned.

He took her to his bedroom, laid her on the hunter-green spread. "Don't move."

He left her feeling bereft, needy and so sensitized she was almost in pain. She watched as he drew his shirt over his head, tossed it on a chair in the corner of the room, then went to the fireplace and added logs to the grate, turning up the gas flame until the wood ignited. The room filled with the scents of apple and smoke.

He glanced back at her, the intensity of his gaze thrilling her. "Reminds me of you. You smell of apples."

"It's my body lotion." Her voice was breathless. She felt funny laying here, waiting for him. But she couldn't have moved if her life depended on it. She wanted him.

And she would have him.

If only for tonight.

He walked toward her and she took the time to admire his body. His stomach was washboard flat—unlike her own. Would he notice the changes in her body? Of course he would. They were pretty obvious.

"Hey. You're not going shy on me, are you?"

She shrugged. "I look a little different than the last time…uh, we were…you know."

His smile was slow and compassionate. And his eyes were like hot chocolate. "You are the sexiest woman I've ever met. I got the better end of the bargain that night in the hotel. This time's for you."

He eased down beside her on the bed and slowly ran his hands over her body, taking his time, removing her clothes a piece at a time, kissing each inch of skin that he revealed.

"Shameless," he murmured when he uncovered her tattoo. "I can't believe I missed this before." His lips caressed the little sunflower on her hip, his tongue tracing the delicate petals, raising goose bumps on her skin. She writhed beneath him, the need to communicate her needs overwhelming, the ability to do so impossible.

His body felt warm and heavy next to her, over her, pressing against her.

She strained against him, lifting her hips off the bed, trying to get closer.

"Easy. Just feel."

She wanted to scream. If she felt any more, she'd surely die.

His palm smoothed over her belly, paying homage to the tight skin that stretched over their baby.

When he looked up at her, met her eyes, the connection and silent communication was profound. And sensual. The combination made her eyes sting.

"I never knew I could want a woman like I want you."

The softness of his words wrapped around her, causing her heart to tumble all the way. It was so easy to get caught up in right now, just this moment, just this exquisite, mind-numbing pleasure. To pretend that the rest of the world didn't exist, that there were no obligations, no children from a previous marriage whose opinions could make or break their relationship.

There were so many factors to consider. And she wished there were none. That the world was theirs to explore, to shape, to do as they wished. She wanted to love and be loved, to surrender body and soul.

But it would be wise to keep a small part of herself back. Otherwise she could break.

"I can feel you thinking, Darcie, and I'm not going to let you do this to us. I'm not going to let you pull back. I'm going to make love to you, slowly, thoroughly like I promised. I'm going to make you so wild, you won't even know your own name. And then I'm going to start all over again."

His fevered, raspy words were the sweetest kind of verbal foreplay. She felt herself teetering on that edge of madness, that precipice that he'd described where she knew nothing but the sensuality of his touch.

He brushed her lips with his, so warm, so smooth, his tongue playing across the seam of her mouth in an erotic dance, asking for and gaining entrance. He took her to those very heights she'd only dreamed about—with just the mere play of his lips. He made her want more, but before those thoughts could coalesce into words, her mind would go blank. She was in his hands, and helpless to participate, to do more than just feel as he'd asked.

"Flynn...for the love of—" She nipped at his shoulder with her teeth, reared up, tried to pull him to her, against her, in her.

"Uh-uh. Not yet."

"You're killing me."

"Mmm. A good kind of killing?" His tongue circled her breast, his fingers dancing over her abdomen, then lower.

She sucked in a breath, arched against his hand.

"Like that?" His finger dipped inside her, stroked, teased, aroused.

She couldn't speak.

He exerted pressure with his thumb and she came apart, screamed. Fisting her hand in his hair, she yanked him to her, ate at his lips, her movements in a frenzy of need. She wouldn't let him put her off. Her legs wrapped around his waist and she rolled with him, reversing their positions, sitting up on top of him, rubbing against him, riding the storm of passion.

Naked, she straddled him, looked down at him through the haze of her desire. "It's your turn now."

His smile was like the wolf in a certain fairy tale. His eyes were hot with promise. And Darcie nearly melted into a pool right there on top of him when he shook his head ever so slightly, hooked his hands at her waist, rolled her onto her back again, raised up over her.

"I told you, this is your time. And I'm not done with you yet."

With single-minded intent, his lips cruised from her neck to her chest, over her belly and lower still.

"Flynn, please."

He'd deliberately misunderstood her, but all of her thoughts stopped at that moment when his lips closed over the very heart of her femininity.

He was as good as his word. He made her wild. And he made her scream. But he never gave her respite. Just when she thought she could take no more, he gave her more, started all over again.

Darcie was mindless and numb. She was sobbing by the time he finally removed his pants. When he entered her, she wasn't one hundred percent sure she even remained conscious.

All she knew was that she was riding one long continuous crest of a climax, with no way to tell when one ended and another began.

It was the sweetest kind of torture, the most exquisite gift. The unselfish giving. Never asking for anything in return. The total focus on her pleasure.

WHEN DARCIE woke the next morning, she wasn't sure how to act. She felt embarrassed, of all things. And that was saying something. She was a woman who was game for just about anything. Yet, last night Flynn had touched and looked at every part of her body—and her soul.

Mercy. She felt herself getting hot all over again.

Still, in the light of day, she was clear-minded—and female—enough to suffer a twinge over what he thought of her body. She was no sexy goddess to begin with, and with her pregnancy beginning to show...well, she couldn't help but wonder what had gone through his mind, whether there had been any comparisons....

She turned her head on the pillow, saw his dark head, his closed eyes, the stubble in his jaw.

She ought to get up, to sneak out of here, to gather her wits before she had to face him.

His eyes opened. "Hi."

Her heart pounded and her face heated. She couldn't seem to speak.

He smiled, pulled her against his chest, kissed her forehead, ran his hand over her hip, pausing over her tattoo. "Marry me."

She stiffened, scooted away.

"Darcie?"

Her clothes were strewn across his bedroom. She didn't have a nightgown in here, either. Dragging the spread off the bed, she wrapped herself in it, walked across the forest-green carpet and picked up her top. "I should shower and get ready for work."

He propped himself up in the bed. "It's Saturday."

"I have some paperwork to do." Nothing pressing, though.

Her heart lurched when he swung his legs over the side of the bed. He was gloriously naked. And aroused. Masculine intent radiated from him like a beacon through a stormy night when he stood.

"Evidently I didn't accomplish my goal last night."

She backed up a step, tripping over the blanket.

"Careful." He kept coming.

"What do you mean?" The dresser was at her back. She didn't have anywhere to go. And did she really want to escape, anyway?

"I mean, that I must not have done something right if you can so easily get out of bed and announce you have to work when we're both clearly naked and free to explore more sensual pleasures."

She'd challenged him and hadn't even meant to. Uh-oh, that meant trouble.

"There are kids in the house."

"Kid. Singular." He stopped in front of her, eased the blanket from her clutching fingers, his brown eyes flaring at the sight of her body. "And she's still asleep." He nodded at the quiet baby monitor on his nightstand.

"Yes, but she won't be much longer. Just think, we'll get started and have to stop."

His lips cruised her jaw, his finger toying with the upper swell of her breast. "That's half the enjoyment. Heightened sensations. If we're interrupted, the nerves will just sing louder and longer until we can put out the fire."

She groaned. "Flynn, don't do this to me. I can't think about sex all day. Especially around the kids."

"Heather's not coming home until late this afternoon. Come back to bed, Darcie."

She wanted to give in. She really did. But he robbed her of good sense when she let him get this close. And the sex was great, sure, but that wasn't reason enough to let him talk her into marriage— which he could likely do if she let herself be seduced so obsessively like he had last night. A woman could only stand firm for so long.

Up against Flynn O'Grady's brand of sexual persuasion, she didn't have a prayer.

"We can't," she said against his mouth.

"We can." He held her in a sensual vise, one arm around her back, his other around her hips, his fingers exploring, arousing, insuring her cooperation.

"You don't play fair."

"I never promised to play fair. Marry me."

"No."

"Then come to bed with me."

"I don't think my system can handle another session like last night."

He smiled against her lips. "I do like those positive strokes." He let the blanket drop to the carpet. His skin was hot against her. His arousal pushed against her. Reaching down, he gripped her thigh and pulled it up to his waist, supporting her with his arm and his thigh.

With her pregnant tummy between them, it should have been an awkward position, but Flynn's sure, masculine hold made it easy, erotic.

He was hard and hot and ready for her. He wanted her as much as she wanted him, that much was obvious.

And suddenly Darcie couldn't remember why she was resisting. There was no reason at the moment why they couldn't enjoy each other. She should hoard these moments, enjoy them, savor them. Because one day very soon, it could all come crashing down over their heads.

It all hinged on his daughter. And though Heather had come to trust Darcie as a friend, the girl was still troubled. She was still raw from losing her mother. It would take very little to push her over the edge.

But for now, there was just Darcie and Flynn. There was just the warmth of their bodies, the tip of his arousal pressing against the core of her femininity.

She slipped her leg higher on his waist, wrapped her arms around his neck and urged him inside of her.

She sucked in a breath, held it, held him. The sensations that built were like a wildfire sweeping through her system. Immediate. Incendiary. She wanted to move, to thrust against him, to create a friction that would drive them both mad.

But he held her hips still, pressed higher, harder, angling their bodies for the maximum sensation and pleasure.

She'd never known stillness could create such an explosion of sensation. She cried out. "Flynn!"

"Shhh. Yes." His breathing heavy, he lifted her other leg, wrapped it around his waist, supporting her entire weight with his hands on her hips. Then he walked to the bed and lowered her without ever breaking the contact of their bodies, following her down, pressing higher, harder, thrusting slowly, steadily, building the momentum, taking her once more to a paradise that most women could only dream about.

His hand slipped between them and caressed her stomach, then lower, finding that sensitive spot that sent her right over the edge of forever.

Just before she tumbled, just before she lost all coherent thought, she heard his voice, raspy, insistent, sure. "You're mine."

MARY BETH PLAYED in the high chair, dropping her cup over the side and eyeing Darcie with a grin. It was a game. "You little stinker." She folded the newspaper she'd been reading, bent and retrieved the cup, set it back on the plastic tray.

"She's a smart cookie," Flynn said. "She knows a person shouldn't have her nose buried in the stock quotes on such a fine Saturday morning."

Darcie rolled her eyes. "In case you hadn't noticed, it's snowing on this fine Saturday morning."

"Yes, and just look how beautiful it is." He sat at the breakfast table, pushed a plate of toast in front of her, then lifted her foot into his lap, massaging through her thick sock.

Darcie nearly purred. This was what life could be like, she thought. Sharing breakfast together. A baby in the high chair. Love in the air. Sultry looks across a plate of toast. Memories, hot and vivid, of a night spent burning up the sheets.

She shook her head, told herself not to get carried away.

"What do you say we take in a matinee this afternoon after we pick up Heather?"

Darcie thought that sounded like a fine idea. Her heart squeezed. "That would be a wonderful father-daughter outing for you and Heather."

He frowned. "It would be a great *family* outing, too."

Darcie pushed away the plate of toast and stood, her gaze focused on the coffeepot. She had a sudden urge for a cup.

Flynn snagged her hand before she could get past him, halting her. He drew her down in his lap. "Don't run from this, Darcie."

She wanted to stay right here in his lap for the rest of her life. But that wasn't possible, much as she wished it were.

She gazed down into his gentle brown eyes, lightly touched the side of his face with the backs of her fingers. Her heart wrenched at the bittersweet sensations that rushed through her veins.

"I can't go to the movies with you, Flynn. I have to be at the hot line this afternoon."

The reminder of why they'd come together again hung between them like a living entity.

And it *was* a living entity—his daughter.

"We need to talk to Heather," he said. "You saw how she was last night. She accepts you, Darcie."

"As a boarder. A friend."

He sighed, placed his hand over her stomach. "This is her sister."

"I know."

"When do you plan to tell your parents?"

She shrugged.

"If I didn't know better, I'd think you were ashamed of me."

"But you *do* know better. I'm just really cautious. The hot line's made me that way. Tammy did. When Heather called that first time, when I realized who she was... It's just so much more complicated. So scary."

He drew her to him, just held her quietly for a moment. "I know you think you know Heather better than me because of your experience with the hot line and the troubled teens you deal with every day, but she's different, Darcie. I have to believe that she is. That she only called you as a means of crying out. That she would never follow through with that threat to run away."

"Oh, I wish it were that easy. And I wish we could know for certain that was true. But we can't. We have to be careful. Our fate isn't up to us."

He rested his palm over her stomach. "What about this baby's fate?"

She didn't have an answer for him. She saw the emotions in his eyes, recognized them as her own, both sadness and fragile hope. It was there in the way he framed her pregnant belly, in the reverent sketch of his lips over the taut skin as he bent his head and softly pressed his mouth against her.

It was in the way he took her hand every time they encountered a step, in the way he watched her, aware yet unconscious of his own solicitude.

Allowing herself this time with Flynn was both joyous and heartbreaking. She wanted a lifetime.

Yet, reality dictated that they might only have a few days.

Tears burned. She stood. "I need to get dressed." She left the room because she just didn't know what else to say. She didn't dare to hope.

THAT EVENING, Heather was bubbling over with plans for the decorations in the auditorium for the Valentine's Day dance.

Flynn noticed that Darcie was quiet and wondered if she'd had a rough case when she'd manned the hot line today. Every time their eyes met, they held for long moments. He wanted to whisk her right upstairs and into his bed. But she was right. They had to be discreet around Heather.

But Heather would have to be told about their situation sooner or later. Darcie was having his baby.

Surely Heather wouldn't take it too badly. The baby would be her sister.

He would have three girls.

That thought just hit him. Boy, would he be outnumbered! And weddings—he'd have to start saving.

"Dad, are you listening? How come you're smiling like that?" Heather glanced from him to Darcie.

"Just feeling good, munchkin."

She rolled her eyes at the endearment. "Darcie, come upstairs and let me show you the really cool dress Liz's mom gave me. Like I couldn't believe she'd even have something like this."

''You mean you thought anybody over the age of twenty-five was an old fogie?''

Heather looked both guilty and horrified that she might have hurt Darcie's feelings.

Darcie laughed. ''Come on. Show me the dress.''

She followed the girl upstairs and sat on the bed. Heather shoved hangers aside in her closet, then withdrew a clingy floor-length dress in blue polyester spandex. Sleeveless with a scooped neck, it fell in a flowing A-line from an empire waist. It was one of those dresses that could go from day to night, the kind of dress that would blend at a summer picnic or an evening garden party—or an eighth-grade dance.

''Liz's mom's got good taste. Maybe I should put her in touch with *my* mom,'' Darcie said, feeling just a pang of envy over the dress. With her tummy pooching out as it was, she couldn't get away with wearing anything clingy. Never mind that the dress had an empire waist. That was only a clever illusion on the designer's part. The dress was made to be clingy and a bit sexy.

Flynn would most likely pitch a fit.

''Do you think Dad will like it?''

Hope was in the girl's voice. Darcie cleared her throat. ''Um, what's not to like?''

Heather rolled her eyes and sat on the bed. ''He hates it when I wear low stuff.''

''Fathers go through a weird stage when their daughters grow boobs.''

Heather giggled. ''You crack me up.'' She

glanced covetingly at Darcie's chest. "I want boobs like yours when I finish growing."

Darcie automatically touched herself, feeling the slight sensitivity from last night's lovemaking. "They're not usually this big. Pregnancy is wonderful for a woman's chest measurement, but hell on the waistline."

Heather's gaze settled on Darcie's stomach, reserve stiffening her shoulders. Darcie had seen that same reaction several times before. A cloud seemed to pass before the girl's eyes every time there was a blatant reminder or mention of pregnancy.

"How come your baby's father isn't around?"

Oh, no. Darcie hadn't meant for the conversation to go in this direction. She wasn't ready to answer these questions. She wanted everything to be right. She wanted to be sure that Heather could handle the answers, that they wouldn't cause harm.

She wanted guarantees where there were none.

"He is… It's complicated." She heard movement at the door, turned.

Flynn stood there with Mary Beth in his arms and he was looking solemn…and scared.

Heather watched them. "You guys are acting weird."

Flynn moved into the room, sat on the bed and reached for his daughter's hand. "Darcie and I have something to tell you," he said softly, carefully. "It's a happy thing, so please—"

"No!" Heather jumped up, backing up a step as though warding off a blow that she couldn't see coming but knew was there. Tears welled in her eyes.

Flynn wanted to cry. By the look on her anguished face, Heather knew without anyone having to say the words. She was a smart girl. Perceptive.

Heather's gaze dropped to Darcie's stomach, then back to her face, then to her dad again. Tears tracked down her cheeks and her fingers closed into fists at her side, trembling, her chin quivering.

"You're…you two… You said you were my friend," she accused Darcie, her voice cracking.

"Oh, honey, I am."

"No. You lied to me."

Darcie reached out, but Heather pulled away. "I didn't lie," she said quietly, dropping her hand, respecting Heather's need for distance.

"You were only pretending to be nice to me because of my dad. Because you wanted him. Not me." Oh, the hurt was stinging. Why did it always feel like this, Heather wondered. Why didn't anybody want her? Why did she always have to take a back seat to her dad or to Mary Beth? Now she'd have to stand in an even longer line because of this new baby. They didn't have to say the words. She could see the truth in their faces.

"That's not true, Heather. You called me, remember? And I've always been there for you."

Heather heard a sadness in Darcie's voice, but she wasn't going to be swayed. She was mad. And she was hurt and confused. It was gross to think about her dad…well, it was just gross. "I told you my name. Didn't you put it together? Figure out that I was related to Dad?''

"Heather," Flynn admonished gently.

"Oh, that's right. Take her side. You always take everybody else's side against me. And what about Mom? You were *married* to her. And you were having Darcie as a girlfriend too? You betrayed Mom!"

Flynn felt his emotions erupt. His jaw clenched as he tried to harness them. Heather's accusation was unfair, but it still hit a nerve. It still made him feel inadequate.

"Your mom left *us,* Heather." He said it softly when he really wanted to shout. And Marsha had been gone a year now. It'd been some nine months since their separation, over five months since her death. That's why he'd been drowning his sorrows that night he'd met Darcie in the bar. He'd just learned of Marsha's death.

"Yeah. She's gone because you got her pregnant!"

With that accusation ringing in the air, Heather ran from the room, leaving Darcie and Flynn staring at one another.

Mary Beth's lip trembled and Flynn hugged her, trying to soothe.

"This is what I was afraid of," Darcie said, shaking.

Flynn's insides were quaking with sick dread. "She loves me, Darcie. I have to believe that. I have to believe that's strong enough to get us through this."

He drew in a breath that actually hurt. My God,

Heather actually blamed him for Marsha getting pregnant. For Mary Beth. No wonder her reaction to Darcie's baby was so strong.

He felt as though this was the most important moment in his life, as though nothing before or after would ever be as difficult, as frightening. Somehow he had to make it right, say it right. Oh, God, what if he blew it?

"Will you take Mary Beth while I go talk to her?"

Darcie nodded and accepted the baby. She was trained to soothe teens in crisis. In this instance, she felt totally ill equipped to handle the job.

And that was upsetting. Because this one really counted. It was personal.

Chapter Eleven

Snow fell outside the window, glittering like fairy dust as it floated past the colored illumination of the landscape lighting that decorated the grounds.

Darcie turned when she heard Flynn come into the family room. "Did you get everything settled?"

Flynn rubbed the back of his neck and lowered himself to the couch, pulling her down beside him. "I never can tell with Heather whether or not anything's *settled*. But we did talk." He held on to her hand and placed it on his thigh, smoothing her tense fingers.

She started to tug away.

"Don't."

"Flynn, she could come down here."

"She won't. She's in bed. And I need you, Darcie. Just...just don't pull away, okay?"

Faced with his weary tone, she didn't have the heart to argue. "Okay." She turned her hand, linked her fingers with his. "Want to talk?"

He shook his head but spoke anyway. "It's like she doesn't want to hang out with me, but she doesn't want anybody else to, either. Does she hate me or something?''

''No, Flynn. She's thirteen. It's written somewhere that girls her age are supposed to treat their fathers this way.''

''Well, it drives me nuts.'' He rested his head against the back of the couch. ''I love these kids with all my heart, Darc, but I hate all this.''

''What?''

''Being a parent. I'm not good at it. I can't wait to see them each day, but then when I do I screw up somehow. Somebody usually ends up yelling, and the dissension and uncertainty are eating me alive. I feel like I'm treading on quicksand and I'm about to get sucked under. Heather can make me feel like a slug with only a look and then Mary Beth starts screaming her lungs out and I start sweating, and I swear I just want to quit.''

''That's normal.''

He shifted his head, looked at her, uncertainty heavy in his eyes. ''Are you sure?''

''As sure as I can be. Aside from the upsets, those kids love you.''

A dimple creased his cheek and his fingers toyed with hers. ''You're right. I think I feel better now.''

She wished she did. ''You just needed to get it out.''

''Yeah, and I appreciate you being here.''

She glanced away. Her house of cards was tumbling, no matter how good a spin Flynn was trying to put on it. Heather was terribly fragile. And because of that, Darcie's ''being here'' wasn't a sure thing. As much as she wanted to believe everything would work out fine, that they'd all live happily ever after, she couldn't be sure. She believed in love, believed that it made a person strong, enabled one to overcome anything. Her family had taught her that.

But you couldn't *make* somebody love you. That was the scary part of this powder keg she'd found herself sitting atop.

"Hey," Flynn said, squeezing her fingers. "Chin up. She'll come around. She has to."

"Don't kid yourself, Flynn. We just told her I'm having your baby. Her sister. Do you expect her to decide to embrace us based on the passage of a few hours or a few days?"

"I will do whatever it takes, Darcie. I'm not going to lose Heather. Or you." Flynn put his arm around her shoulders, drew her to him, pressed his lips against her forehead.

"I swear I can watch Heather's eyes brim with tears one minute, then see her dancing with a teddy bear the next. She's not a girl to carry grudges. She processes information, weighs it, then she accepts."

"I know she's a good girl, smart and mature for her age. But we've put a lot on her, Flynn. And she's still raw from her mom's death."

"She doesn't blame you for that. She blames me."

"No. There's no blame. Only hurt."

"Marsha was good at dishing out hurt." He raked a hand through his hair, leaned his head back against the couch again and stared at the ceiling. "When we were first married, she stayed home and took care of things here. I probably took a lot of what she did for granted. I was busy building my career. But she said that's how she wanted it. Then Heather was born.

"Marsha had been doing charity work and one of the donors admired her organizational skills, felt she had what it took to excel in marketing. He offered her a job. Marsha was flattered. I was worried at first, because of how it would affect me."

He ran a hand over his face. "Selfish, huh?"

Darcie didn't comment; she just squeezed his knee.

"Anyway, Marsha, ever the efficient one, hired a nanny for Heather. The household ran smoothly, our daughter was well taken care of, meals were on the table and the laundry and house was kept in top-notch form."

He reached over and smoothed the line between Darcie's brows. "I know, I sound like a total chauvinist pig. I didn't realize it then, but maybe that's what I'd turned into. I was the one who wanted the family. But I didn't think that it would be my responsibility to take care of it. I'd been raised to believe that was the woman's job. My mom did it."

"And your dad?" she asked.

"He worked and paid the bills. Moved us out of the burg and into Princeton. Mom tried to keep up, but the country club set wasn't really her cup of tea. She attended the functions, did the charities, but she was happiest at home. Dad outgrew her. He took off when I was eighteen."

"Are you still in contact with him?"

"He had a heart attack at forty-eight and died. That's when I took a good look at my life, at the fast track I was living and decided that I needed to slow down. That *we* needed to slow down. To be a family. But by then, Marsha was on her way up the promotion ladder at her company and loving it. She'd been groomed to be the perfect wife and asset to her man. She found out that she liked being her own woman. And I could appreciate that. It was her falling in love with her boss I couldn't handle."

"Oh, Flynn."

He tried to shrug it off. "I think I knew it all along. We'd taken a weekend to try to focus on us, on our marriage. Marsha's heart wasn't in it. Hell, maybe mine wasn't, either. That's the weekend Mary Beth was conceived."

She tightened her hand around his. He liked the link, the support. Seemed he was doomed to conceive children under less-than-ideal circumstances. He wondered if she was thinking the same thing.

But regardless of the circumstances, he loved Mary Beth with all his heart. And he loved the little girl Darcie carried in her womb, too.

"Marsha didn't want to go through the baby stage of motherhood again, but I talked her into it. I was determined at that point to make a go of the marriage. For Heather's sake, Marsha agreed. She took a leave of absence during the last few months of her pregnancy and even let the nanny go. It all seemed like it was before, and I guess I convinced myself that we'd make it work."

He sighed, leaned forward. "She left when Mary Beth was a month old. Went back to work and served me with legal separation papers. I knew it was final then. And I gave up all hope. Any feelings I had for her were pretty much gone by that time anyway. Still, I was left with the kids."

"Did you hire the nanny back?"

"No. My mom came to the rescue. Moved in and took over. And I fell right back into my old routine, letting her take care of the house and kids—just like I had with Marsha in the early days of our marriage."

He glanced at her. "I don't imagine I'm painting myself in a very good light in your eyes, but I promise I've learned a lot of lessons lately."

She frowned, and he touched her tummy. "I'm not the arrogant guy I used to be, Darc."

Her breath hitched and her eyes widened. He liked the way his touch affected her. It made him feel like a man. And lately, that was a feeling that didn't come too often, what with teenage woes and baby diapers and tears. Still, he was doing an adequate job in the apron department, and finding that he actually got a great deal of satisfaction out of it.

"When Aunt Lois broke her hip, Mom needed to go to her. That threw me back into a tizzy. I was all alone with the girls. And I'd never had Mary Beth on my own before. I was scared to death and making a mess out of everything. That's when I basically felt pushed to the wall and that's why I agreed to go to The Daddy Club when Ross called."

She glanced at him, her look filled with both amusement and reserve.

His smile was knowing. "I never even knew I'd been maneuvered. By you."

She shrugged. "From what Heather said about you, I knew you were salvageable. You just needed some help."

"You knew more about me than just what Heather had said. We'd already been naked together."

Her cheeks heated. It was charming. Because Darcie wasn't a woman given to embarrassment easily.

"I've already admitted to taking a bit of advantage of you that night," she said. "But you're right. I knew you had a good heart."

"And good other things?" He leaned into her, wanting to get closer. She retreated. He let her get away with it this time.

"That night at the hotel, I was trying to convince myself that I hadn't been to blame for my failed marriage. I was feeling bruised. Marsha had died just the week before. I didn't want to be at the convention, but I was a speaker and couldn't get out of it."

"And I took advantage of you," Darcie repeated.

He looked at her for a long moment. "No. I believe it was the other way around."

She shook her head. "You didn't even know who I was at first."

"Yes, I did."

"You did?"

"Darcie Moretti. How could I ever forget those sexy freckles? That great laugh?"

She ducked her head, knew they were treading on dangerous ground here. Flynn O'Grady could make her melt with a word or a look.

She scooted to the edge of the couch and stood. "I think I better take these freckles to bed before we get in trouble."

He reached for her hand, stopped her exit. "If you'd marry me, we wouldn't have all these problems you're inventing. We'd have the right to neck on the couch or go upstairs to bed together."

"No, we wouldn't. We still wouldn't have the right to hurt Heather."

"We didn't do this to her deliberately, Darcie. I'm betting you're wrong about her acceptance. I'm betting that she'll bounce back. She's crazy about you."

Oh, she wished she could be sure. "When it comes to the kids, I'm not a betting kind of gal."

She moved away from him, stopped when he softly called her name. "All this doesn't change the fact that you're having my baby."

"I know."

"I'm not going to let you pull away from me."

"I know that, too." Her throat ached and tears stung. "But it just might not be up to you."

She made it to the bottom stair, paused when he came up behind her. "Promise me something?"

She turned to him and nearly lost her good intentions. He looked like a man who could use a pair of arms to hold him. And she desperately wanted those arms to be hers. "What?"

"Promise that you'll at least give our family a chance. That you won't jump the gun. Give Heather a chance to come around."

She rested her palm against his cheek, felt herself drowning in his eyes. "That's exactly why I'm still here."

DARCIE FELT like she was walking on eggshells the next morning. Her first instinct was to grab her computer and her briefcase and head out of the house, to hide out in her office. But as uncomfortable as she felt, that would be the wrong thing to do to Heather. The girl's mother had put work before her family's feelings.

Darcie would stick it out, no matter how uncomfortable.

Flynn was at the stove, an apron tied around his waist, a skillet of eggs sizzling over a too-high flame. Mary Beth squealed from her high chair and upended a bowl of oatmeal on her head.

Flynn swore and the spatula went flying, splattering runny egg yokes over the wall as he dove for the cereal bowl before it hit the floor. "No, baby! The food goes in your mouth."

A curl of steam escaped the toaster and the smell of burning bread filled the air. With a hand full of mushy oatmeal, he abandoned that disaster and charged for the toaster, slapping the lever, sending blackened wheat bread sailing out of the slots. He made a grab for the bread, then yelped when it burned his fingers.

Heather giggled from her place at the table. He stopped, shot her a look. "You could help, you know." A grin tugged at his freshly shaven cheeks.

She shrugged, got up and tore off half a roll of paper towels, mopping up the mess on Mary Beth's high chair tray.

Darcie still hovered by the doorway. Like she'd predicted, Heather didn't appear to be angry with her dad. The love was there and evident.

But that didn't mean it would extend to Darcie. Nor were there guarantees that the mood wouldn't undergo a severe chill if she breached the family sanctuary.

Taking a breath, she stepped forward, lowered the burner under the skillet, picked up the spatula and rinsed it at the sink.

Heather paused. So did Flynn. Darcie felt like the air could be cut with a knife. It was thick with smoke and emotions.

Then the fire alarm shrilled, making everybody jump and scaring Mary Beth into tears. Like an old comedy, the kitchen erupted with activity once more.

Flynn grabbed a broom and smacked the smoke detector. Its plastic cover went sailing. Heather covered her baby sister's body as though a bomb had exploded. The kitten chose that moment to race into the room, paws swiping like a seasoned hockey player, batting at the smoke detector cover as though it had been tossed just for her benefit. She skidded in the slick oatmeal, lost traction and sprawled under the table.

Darcie couldn't help it. The scene was such a disaster, she laughed.

Flynn whirled around. "You think you could do a better job in here?"

Heather actually looked stunned that he could voice such an inane question, then she rolled her eyes and glanced at Darcie.

Darcie was determined to act normal, but she was ever watchful of the teen, gauging her mood. It gave her heart a glad leap when Heather smiled as though they were on the same side, as though being the females in the room they were the only ones with a clue.

And that didn't appear to be too far off base if one were to objectively look at the sorry state of the kitchen. But Flynn was trying. And she wouldn't burst his bubble. He looked a little wilted.

"I'm sure you're doing a fine job, but it always goes a little smoother with some help." She scooped up the kitten and put it in its basket, then scraped the eggs from the bottom of the pan. A wet sponge took care of the runny yokes decorating the tile backsplash, and an open window let out the worst of the smoke.

Baby Kitty was doing a fairly decent job of licking herself clean, but Darcie shut her in the laundry room just in case. No sense having oatmeal tracked all over the carpet.

"I don't think you're gonna make it to Wednesday,'' Heather muttered, a dimple peeking out in her cheek even though she concentrated on not smiling.

''What's that supposed to mean?'' Flynn asked, his tone teasing even though he tried to act put upon. When he'd lost control in the kitchen, he'd felt like screaming right along with Mary Beth and the fire alarm, but watching his daughter and Darcie work in tandem, feeling the utter sense of family, gave him a boost.

This could be their life. A happy life. Not perfect, by any stretch, but a good life. Darcie was great with his kids. They responded to her. All it had taken was her happy laughter to change the mood, to avert disaster.

Had this been Marsha, they would have each tried to blame the other and ended up in a fight that would chill the atmosphere for days.

''Wednesday's The Daddy Club night,'' Heather said, pretending to concentrate on cleaning up her sister. Mary Beth thought it was a great game to keep her little fingers closed into fists with mushy oatmeal squeezing out the cracks. ''Gross, Mary Beth. Open your hands.''

Mary Beth babbled and giggled.

''Are you insinuating I could use some lessons?''

Darcie laughed, then clapped a hand to her mouth, though anyone with a set of eyes could see she wasn't repentant.

Flynn glared.

Heather did a much better job acting solemn. ''Look around the room, Dad.''

He grinned. ''Looks pretty bad. But I don't think

cooking classes include babies slinging oatmeal right in the middle of the process. You have to admit that would tax even Martha Stewart.''

Heather rolled her eyes again, this time to cover her amusement, rather than in teenage disgust. The phone rang and she abandoned the oatmeal cleanup, rushing across the kitchen and snatching up the receiver.

Flynn brushed up next to Darcie. ''See?'' he said softly. ''You were worried for nothing.''

He was talking about Heather's acceptance of them. ''Don't jump the gun, okay? Let's take it slow.''

He glanced at her stomach. ''Not too slow. I want her to have my name.''

Darcie automatically placed a hand on her stomach. ''She can have your name anyway.''

''But I want you, too.''

''Dad?''

They both jumped and turned toward Heather. Their voices had been too low to be overheard, but not the emotions on their faces.

Heather didn't appear to have noticed, though. ''Ruth Naomi wants to know if you know how to put up a towel bar.''

''Yes. Why?''

Heather's attention was snagged for another moment as she cuddled the phone like a cherished friend and listened to what the caller was saying. Then she shifted the mouthpiece and said. ''Are you any good at it?''

''Who are you talking to?'' Flynn asked.

Heather rolled her eyes. "Ruth Naomi. I told you. Are you any good at it?"

"Here, let me talk to her." He held out his hand for the receiver."

Heather frowned. "Wait," she said, dodging her father. Then she grinned. "Do you want me to tell him *that?*" Her grin widened and she turned her eyes to Flynn. "Ruth Naomi said quit acting like a donkey's patootie and answer the question."

Flynn held back his own grin. Ruth Naomi Steadwell had a fresh mouth on her, and claimed at her age there was no changing. "I appreciate the restraint on language, Ruth Naomi," he said, raising his voice so she could hear through the phone. "And yes, I'm pretty good at towel bars."

Heather listened and giggled. "Yeah, he does that macho man thing when he brags." To Flynn, she said, "Can you teach a class for Women in Hardware Wednesday night?"

Flynn looked at Darcie.

"Why are you looking at me?" she asked. "I don't know how to hang a towel bar."

His expression cleared. "No? Then I guess you ought to attend my class. Heather, tell Ruth Naomi I'll be there. Do I need to bring anything?"

"Did you hear him?" Heather asked into the receiver. "Okay. I'll tell him." She shrugged, glanced at Darcie and Flynn, and turned her back. "Okay. Okay. Mmm-hmm. Bye." She hung up the phone. "She said the ladies' class will be first, then you can go do the Daddy Club thing. She has all the stuff you'll need. Just bring your brains and brawn."

"WITH AGE AND USE, the hole can get too big, become sloppy, and no amount of screwing will make it stay in."

"A few dozen Kegel exercises should fix that up. Practice them myself," Marge commented, eliciting a round of gasps and laughter.

Flynn was sweating—never mind that there was snow falling outside and that the interior of the hardware store was a comfortably chilly sixty-eight degrees. Standing in front of a group of women intent on heckling him had that effect.

And he noticed that his daughter and Darcie were immensely enjoying his flustered state.

"What's a Kegel?" Heather asked.

"Never mind!" Flynn said, a bit too loudly, shooting Ruth Naomi a look.

"Don't look at me," Ruth said. "It's your job to teach about these things. And there's nothing in the world wrong with a little conversation to go along with towel bar instruction."

"Yeah, Daddy—"

Darcie leaned over and whispered the answer in his daughter's ear. Heather's eyes widened, and her cheeks blossomed with color as she giggled.

Flynn dropped his chin to his chest, the Molly screw and towel bar forgotten in front of him. "Ladies, please, can we get back to the lesson?"

Just then, a man in a tuxedo waltzed into the room, a bad-boy grin on his handsome face. Micah Steadwell. Ross Steadwell's brother—Ruth Naomi's son. Flynn figured he ought to just pack up his tools and call it a night.

"Sounds like my kind of class. You teaching the birds and the bees, O'Grady?"

Micah Steadwell, former rock-and-roll musician and now owner of The Knight Club, a great little supper club in town, plucked Mary Beth out of Ruth Naomi's arms, perching her on one arm as though he handled baby girls every day of his life. He was a natural at it, having had a lot of practice with Ross's kids.

Flynn cocked a brow. "No. Towel bars. I'll leave the sex ed to you playboys."

Micah covered Mary Beth's ears. "Have a care for the age of your audience, pal."

Flynn knew he'd never regain control of his class—not that he'd had any control to begin with. "As I was saying before the, uh—"

"The Kegels," Ula Mae supplied helpfully.

"Thank you, Ula Mae." He absolutely wasn't going to take the bait. "If your screw's stripped out of the wall, you can replace it with a toggle bolt, or make the hole larger and put in a plastic shield to screw into, or use a Molly. That's my preference and what I'll be showing you."

"How to screw Molly?"

"Molly is a screw."

"The boy's a little crass, but he's great to look at, don't you think?" Ula Mae said, cutting her eyes at Darcie.

Darcie put up her hands. "Don't you dare drag me into this." She laughed and tried to make her expression stern.

Marge elbowed Ula Mae lightly, sharing a grin.

Flynn looked out at the sea of faces. The back door opened and the men starting arriving for The Daddy Club meeting. Great. If his face got any hotter, he'd catch fire. He couldn't remember ever being so uncomfortable, so embarrassed.

Then he saw the humor in it, the looks that passed back and forth between Ruth Naomi and Ula Mae and Marge. He should have spotted it sooner. They were matchmaking. Egging him on. Trying to get Darcie involved, too.

And he might just relax and go with it if it wasn't for the presence of his daughters.

He picked up the awl, opened his mouth, only to be interrupted again. This time by Micah.

"Hey, who's the cute little blonde in the audience?" He gave Heather a wink. "She looks too young for this geriatric class, if you ask me."

Ruth Naomi smacked him on the arm, addressed the class. "It's his father's fault he's such an irreverent boy. And Heather O'Grady is much too savvy to let his disrespect rub off." She managed to tease and introduce in one smart-mouth sentence.

Micah grinned.

"I get a little rowdy around the smell of your muffins." He kissed his mother on the cheek. "They bring out the best and the worst in me. How about it, sweetheart?" he said to Heather. "Want to join me in raiding the kitchen?"

Though Micah was close to Flynn in age, he was a handsome flirt, possessing a young-at-heart aura that would cause any girl's heart to flutter. Young or old.

Heather shrugged and stood, looking down at Darcie as if for permission.

"You'll be safer," Darcie said. "In fact I might join you."

The sexual innuendoes zinging in this room were adding way too much fuel to her fantasies and her memories.

Chapter Twelve

"Holy smoke!" Flynn dropped the plastic baby and leaped back, using his sleeve to swipe at the water dripping from his face. He'd sweated through the teasing of the Women in Hardware class, and now The Daddy Club meeting was promising to further his embarrassment.

Ross Steadwell—who still led the class since it was his brainchild to begin with—laughed along with the rest of the men and shook his head. "Congratulations, buddy, you just dropped your kid on his head. Better call the medics." Ross aimed his water gun and gave another squirt.

Flynn dodged the second stream of water and picked up the doll from the floor. "I'd have thought marriage to Elaine would encourage you to grow up, but I see there's no hope."

Ross grinned. "I'll have you know Elaine loves every inch of my playfulness. And you still need to address the fact that you tossed the baby."

"Give me a break. My experience is with girl

babies. They don't shoot water like that during a diaper change.''

''Yes, well, I'm sure you're adept at diapering little girls, but you never know when you might encounter a boy baby. You do plan on having more children, am I right?''

Flynn glared at his friend, knowing full well that he was getting a dig in about Darcie—and the lack of a wedding ring on her finger. ''I'm working on it, okay? And it's a girl.''

''Who's a girl?'' Aaron Bradley asked. He was new to The Daddy Club—a billionaire CEO who'd recently inherited his nephews.

Flynn realized he'd just put his foot in it. ''The doll,'' he lied. ''It's a girl doll and it shouldn't be peeing straight up.'' He passed it over to Aaron.

Aaron tossed it back, but Flynn sidestepped. Bob, a technician at Data, Ink. where Elaine Steadwell worked, made a desperate dive for the doll, catching it before it hit the floor.

''Hell on fire.'' Out of breath, he glared at Flynn and the rest of The Daddy Club attendees. ''I've got a six-month-old who's not much bigger than this doll. You guys are gonna give me nightmares.''

''If you've got a six-month-old, then you probably need the diapering practice,'' Flynn said.

''Of course I need the practice. That's the whole reason I'm here at The Daddy Club. I can't seem to accomplish these diaper changes without puking all over the place.''

''Yo, Mom!'' Ross shouted across the room.

"Yes, my handsome son?" she yelled back, her voice husky and deep.

"Tell Micah to quit fooling around in the kitchen and bring us a jar of spicy mustard." He turned back to The Daddy Club group. "One poopy diaper coming up."

Flynn made another swipe at his wet face and grinned. He figured he'd gotten off light with the water. Much better than the alternative that Bob was about to tackle. Already the guy was turning a little green around the gills.

Aaron Bradley shoved his hands in his pockets, a playboy smile on his handsome features. "I was prepared to be embarrassed tonight, thinking this would be a touchy-feely sort of meeting."

"And now?" Flynn asked.

"You guys are pretty out of control." His grin widened. "My kind of people. But although diapering classes are all well and good, I could do with some pointers on communicating with kids on the tougher issues. I'm a whiz when it comes to playing with them, but talking about fears and stuff, well I'm over my head."

Flynn did a credible imitation of Heather and rolled his eyes. "Don't look at me to lead that class, buddy. I've got a teen who lets me know on a daily basis that I don't have a clue about communication."

Aaron looked so disappointed, Flynn clapped him on the shoulder. "Not to worry. Ross Steadwell got his two little kids through the death of their mom.

He can probably supply some input and lead a fairly lively discussion on the subject.''

Micah swaggered over and produced the requested mustard, then moved next to Flynn. "Not gonna stand over there and get closer instruction?'' he asked.

"I've just been shot in the eye with a squirt gun by your wise-guy brother. I'm keeping my distance, thanks. Besides, I've got a one-year-old still in diapers. This is one area where I excel.''

Micah nodded. "Mary Beth. Right. She's a cutie. And that Heather's gonna be a heartbreaker.''

Flynn groaned. "Don't even start, okay?''

"Backing off,'' Micah said with a soft laugh. "Heads up.''

Flynn glanced in the direction of Micah's gaze in time to see Ruth Naomi streaking across the room with a trash can and thrusting it into Bob's hands. She then grabbed Ross by the arm and dragged him out of The Daddy Club circle, stopping next to Flynn and Micah and Aaron.

"I think you boys ought to call it a night.''

"Looks like everybody feels the same,'' Ross said, watching as the men scattered. "Sheesh, I had no idea a little spicy mustard would cause such a reaction.'' He gave an experimental squirt with the toy gun just for the hell of it.

"Give me that thing.'' Ruth Naomi took the gun away and tucked it in her pocket. "The poor guy told you he tosses his cookies every time he tries a diaper change. You should have gone easier on him.''

"It was only mustard," Flynn, Ross and Micah said in unison. Aaron, apparently the only wise one in the group, remained silent.

Just for pure fun, Ruth Naomi raised the squirt gun and drenched them all. Then, as though she hadn't just done it, she asked Flynn, "So, where are you taking Darcie for Valentine's Day?"

"You're seeing Darcie?" Micah asked, wiping his face on his tuxedo sleeve. "Cool."

"I'm working on it," Flynn said, glancing across the room to where Darcie stood by the coffee bar. She had Mary Beth on her lap and Heather at her shoulder listening attentively to whatever tale Marge and Ula Mae were spinning. Something inside Flynn softened and clutched.

Those three females were his family. And he loved them.

His heart lurched and his breath caught in his lungs.

Ruth Naomi thumped him on the back. "Swallow the wrong way?" she asked, eyeing him shrewdly.

"Flynn's having trouble romancing Darcie," Ross supplied helpfully.

"Thank you, Ross, for sharing that. I feel so adequate now."

"Hmm. Sounds like you need a dating club as well as a daddy club," Micah said.

Flynn was secure enough to take the teasing, but he put up a front anyway. "You know, three Steadwells at once ganging up on my ego is a bit much."

"Hey, we love to offer advice. And with Darcie

being pregnant and all, she needs extra romancing. Her hormones are obviously delicate.''

Ruth Naomi smacked him. ''I taught you better than to make male remarks like that!''

Micah grinned cheekily and Ross had the good sense to keep his face composed. Aaron discreetly retreated a step. None of them let on, but the woman could terrify them.

''Darcie's hormones aside, Micah does have an excellent suggestion. And Valentine's Day is meant to be spent in a dimly lit, romantic place. I have to say that Micah's supper club fills the bill.''

''Mmm, and speaking of romance...,'' Ross said, his gaze fixed on the door, his steps automatically moving toward his wife. Elaine Steadwell smiled and made a grab for the two little kids she'd just herded into Hardware and Muffins.

Flynn watched Ross cross the room as though being pulled by a magnet, noting the utterly profound look of love on his friend's face.

Envy settled on him like a heavy shroud when Ross and Elaine met halfway across the room, touched, kissed.... The two displayed an aura of radiance even a blind man would see.

Flynn didn't realize he'd sighed until he heard Micah do the same.

Both men straightened their posture and cleared their throats.

''Come by the club about seven,'' Micah said, shoving his hands in his tuxedo pockets. ''I'll set you up with the VIP treatment.''

Flynn nodded and glanced once more at Ross

Steadwell and his family. The children weren't Elaine's by birth but you'd never know. Elaine loved them.

Just like Darcie loved his children, Flynn thought. It could work, he told himself. It *would* work.

Now he just needed to convince Darcie of that.

DARCIE STROKED the velvety petals of the red roses lying on the table, their perfume filling the air. Not a single thorn studded any of the two dozen long stems.

"They're so beautiful," she said.

Flynn's smile was slow and sexy in the shadowy lighting of the supper club. "Not as beautiful as you. You're radiant tonight, Darc."

She looked away, flustered, unsure how to accept his compliments. The urge to tug at the scoop neck of her dress was strong. He was making her a nervous wreck.

The fact that her mother was baby-sitting Flynn's kids and that this was an actual date made her heart pound and her palms damp.

Needing a distraction, she breathed a sigh of relief when Micah, looking like a millionaire playboy in his jet-black tuxedo, approached their table.

"Ah, the Valentine couple. Everything okay with your dinners?" Micah asked.

"Excellent," Flynn said. "Join us for a bit?"

"Thanks, but no. I've got paperwork to do in the back. I just wanted to make sure your meal and service was satisfactory."

"It's great."

"Good. Enjoy. Dance a little. Cherie's a legend when it comes to smoky love songs." Micah glanced at the singer, then shoved his hand in his pocket, jingling his change. "I just wish she wouldn't try to sing them for me," he muttered.

"She's gorgeous," Darcie said, envying the woman her creamy skin and slender waistline.

"Mmm. That she is. But she'd break my heart for sure." His tone was teasing, but there was a restless flare in his eyes, almost as though he was dodging the woman or something. Micah waved and beckoned to a man across the room.

"Is that Aaron Bradley?" Flynn asked.

"Sure is."

"He's new in town," Flynn said to Darcie. "Came to The Daddy Club the other night."

"I remember seeing him." Who wouldn't remember, she thought. Every woman in the restaurant followed him with her eyes. He had a presence about him that radiated both authority and sex appeal. A potent combination. Nearly as potent as Flynn's.

Flynn stood and shook hands with Aaron. "Bradley. Good to see you again." He introduced Darcie.

"Are you here for the excellent food?" she asked, accepting his hand, charmed by the twinkle in his eye. This was a man who knew how to flirt. Too bad it was wasted on her.

"That and the entertainment. I've become a fan of Micah's."

"You'll have to settle for Cherie tonight," Micah said. "I'm taking the evening off."

"No hardship there. Cherie's dynamite." Aaron

turned to Flynn. "I didn't mean to intrude on your evening, but I wondered if we could exchange business cards and perhaps set up a meeting for next week? I've bought a piece of property outside of town and I need to discuss having some plans drawn up for a house."

"Sure thing." Flynn handed over his card. "I'll look forward to getting together."

"Right. Nice meeting you, Darcie." Aaron moved off, and for a minute Darcie watched him, wondering at the sadness she'd glimpsed in his eyes. For a big man, he moved with surprising elegance.

Micah brushed a kiss on Darcie's cheek and shook Flynn's hand. "Glad you both made it to the club. I'll see you later."

When Micah left, Darcie fidgeted in her chair. The room was dark and romantic, just as Ruth Naomi had indicated. Candlelight flickered on the tables and refracted off the crystal goblets.

She raised her water glass and took a sip. She didn't know why she was so nervous with Flynn tonight. But there was something different about him. A flirtatious air. A watchfulness.

An intensity that shook her to her toes.

She glanced up and caught him staring. "What?"

"You're stunning."

She nearly laughed out loud. "I've never been stunning in my life."

He took her hand, pressed his lips to her knuckles.

The action was charming and old-fashioned and nearly melted Darcie's bones. She had an urge to snatch up her water glass again and gulp the liquid to quench the fire.

Instead she stared back at him, held by his gaze, unable to release the breath suspended in her lungs.

The moment spun out. Silver clinked against china and crystal. A low murmur of conversation buzzed, blending with the sultry tone of Cherie's voice as she sang about angels and heros.

"Dance with me," Flynn said, standing and pulling her up with him.

"We shouldn't be doing this."

"Oh, yes we should."

He took her in his arms, eased her up against his body. His leg slipped between hers, pressing ever so slightly, ever so suggestively.

Darcie drew in another long breath, felt her pulse pound in every secret place on her body. "Flynn…"

"Shh. Dance with me. Feel me." His hand at the small of her back urged her closer still, so sure, so masculine.

And she did feel him. All of him. From knees to chest, they moved as one, rubbed, teased. And all the while he watched her.

She couldn't hold his gaze any longer. If it weren't for his firm support, she'd have slid right down into a puddle at his feet.

Oh, this was pure torture.

And pure bliss.

His lips feathered against her hair, his breath puffing against her temple. His hands came around to the sides of her breasts, smoothing upward, raising her arms until they were wrapped around his neck.

"Flynn…"

"I know. We're in public. But this is the day for lovers. And that's what we are, Darc."

"No."

"Yes. And I want more."

She didn't want to argue with him. And she didn't want to talk anymore. She just wanted to feel. To dream. To visualize what their future might be.

For a little while, she wanted to set aside the uncertainty and just pretend.

"Marry me," he whispered in her ear.

"Hush. You're spoiling the mood."

"But—"

She pressed a finger over his lips and dropped her forehead against his neck. Marriage to Flynn O'Grady was her heart's desire. That she wasn't absolutely certain it was truly in the cards for them made her soul cry.

His tongue traced her fingers, sending her heart rate soaring. She'd never wanted a man so badly in her life. Her whole body ached with the want, pulsed with desire.

She could barely draw a breath, but she gave it a good shot anyway. Leaning back just enough to look at him, she said, "Let's get out of here."

He didn't have to be asked twice.

Holding her close, as though he feared she'd disappear if he allowed any space between them, he led her off the dance floor, tossed onto the table enough cash to cover their meals, then snagged her purse off the chair. Darcie snatched up her long-stem roses and allowed him to hustle her outside.

The night air was bracingly cold, the sky inky black and clear of clouds. But even the near freezing temperatures couldn't cool the fire raging inside her. She nearly whimpered when he crushed her to him and kissed her before they could even get to the car.

"I'll never make it home," Flynn said. He glanced around, pulled her by the hand and half sprinted with her across the parking lot.

Darcie saw the hotel and sighed in relief.

He glanced down at her.

"Yes," she said, picking up the pace. "Absolutely yes."

From then on, time seemed a blur. Flynn got them checked into the hotel. She barely had time to appreciate the beautiful antique decor of the hotel or the room before she was in his arms again, kissing him as though there was no tomorrow.

He took the roses from her hand, and tossed them toward the bed.

She felt wild, in a hurry. She jerked his jacket off his shoulders, yanked at his tie, all the while trying to keep her lips pressed to his. Throwing her arms back, she shook off her own coat, then moaned when his hands found and caressed her breasts.

"Oh. So good."

"Mmm, yes. And we'd better slow down."

"No. Gotta hurry." She pulled his belt, fumbled with the hook on his dress pants, managed to get his shirttail untucked and his zipper down before he stopped her.

"Uh-uh. It's Valentine's Day. We'll have a little romance, if you please."

She giggled at the mock-earnest expression on his face. "Afraid I won't respect you in the morning?"

"Exactly."

"Not that we can stay here until morning."

The kids were spending the night at Darcie's parents house but they'd still have to call and tell them where they were, in case of emergency. And he'd sooner die. He looked slyly at Darcie.

"Don't look at me. *I'm* not calling them."

He smiled and pressed a kiss to the side of her mouth then slowly slipped the low-cut knit bodice of her dress over her shoulders. "You just don't want to face Grandma Connor's comments."

"Neither do you." She pulled her arms free of the dress's sleeves.

"True. But I do want to make slow love to you."

"Yes. I like the sound of that. As long as I can love you back."

"Do you?" he asked softly, his brown eyes holding hers.

"What?"

"Love me back."

He'd caught her off guard with that. And to admit to her feelings would give him a leverage that she'd not be able to resist.

More than anything she wanted to accept his marriage proposal, to believe that their futures were meant to be.

But she still needed guarantees.

And she still didn't have those guarantees.

So she chose to deliberately misunderstand him. With her lips trailing down his body and her hands following, she slowly sank to her knees, then looked up at him. "Just watch me love you back...."

THE ENTIRE MORETTI household was in the kitchen, the smell of pancakes filling the house.

Flynn helped Darcie off with her coat and hung it on the hall tree by the front door. "Sounds like there's more chaos in there than usual," he commented.

"That's because the girls are here." She started to run her hands through her hair, then remembered she'd put it in a braid. "We should have picked them up last night. I feel guilty."

Alone in the front hallway, he took the opportunity to press a kiss to her temple. "You look beautiful."

"Behave." The baby in her womb evidently responded to her emotions and gave a tumble. She put her hand on her stomach for just a moment.

Flynn automatically stepped forward, his hands covering hers, his handsome features worried. "Are you okay? Is something wrong?"

"Everything's fine. The baby's just stretching."

The look on his face was so soft, so caring, so loving, she had to look away. "We better get in there."

Turning, she headed across the front hall to the kitchen.

The noise level in the hub of the Moretti household was a muted roar, with several different conversations going on at the same time, as well as the sound of happy laughter and baby babble.

The voices came to an abrupt halt when they entered, making Darcie feel like everybody knew exactly what she and Flynn had done last night.

Lord, *she* couldn't believe what they'd done. She'd never be able to look at a red rose in exactly the same way again without feeling the erotic blush of desire.

Several expressions crossed Heather's face as her gaze touched on Darcie's stomach, then at both Darcie and Flynn. There was hurt, uncertainty and then a lightning-swift transformation into youthful happiness.

Grandma Connor and Darcie's mom both had brows raised and a look that said they each couldn't wait to get her alone.

Uh-oh.

The moment ended and activity resumed, everyone picking up where they'd left off, talking at once.

"You're in time for breakfast," Rose said, bustling around the kitchen. "Sit." She brushed by Darcie, squeezed her daughter's arm and gave an approving nod in Flynn's direction. "You had a good time?"

"Yes," Darcie said, trying not to meet anyone's eyes directly, trying to gauge Heather's mood. It felt as though there was a puzzle piece missing, and she wasn't quite sure what it was.

"Good. And you talked?"

Much more than talked. "Yes, that's usually what you do when you go to dinner with somebody." Darcie noticed that her father was giving Flynn one of his cop looks. She moved next to her mother at the stove and whispered. "Is everything okay here?"

"We know about the baby," Rose whispered back. "I mean about the father. Heather let it slip. She didn't know we didn't know. I can't believe you don't tell your mother these things."

"Mom, not now, okay?"

Rose glanced back at the table. Flynn had spoken to Johnny Moretti and the two men had excused themselves from the room. "Your father is pleased, although he's putting on a front with that mean expression."

Darcie started to go join the men, just in case her mother was wrong and things got out of hand, but Rose stopped her with a hand on her arm. "Let them be. They'll be fine. Your Heather is fragile, though. She cares a great deal for you, but there's so much going on inside her."

"I know." Darcie picked up a plate of pancakes and carried them to the table.

"How come you're not at work?" Heather asked.

"I took the day off."

"Late night?" Heather gave a cocky teenage look with both brows lifted. School was closed today for a teachers' meeting.

"We had a nice dinner at Micah's club," she answered, ignoring the challenge. Her palms were sweating though. Heather had been through plenty lately. With the news that Darcie was going to have Flynn's baby, and then Darcie and Flynn going out on a date, Darcie had been afraid it would be too much for the girl.

But Heather was half in love with Darcie's family, practically adopting them as surrogate grandparents. She'd been eager to spend the night.

Heather sighed and sat down. Ducking her head, she said quietly, "I didn't know your mom didn't know about the baby...and my dad. I didn't mean to tell on you."

"That's okay." Darcie placed her hand over Heather's, encouraged when the girl didn't jerk away. "It was wrong of me not to say anything. I might be over thirty, but I still make bad decisions. I still worry about disappointing my parents."

"You do?" Heather seemed surprised. Darcie realized they'd touched on a commonality.

"Yeah, I do. But I screwed up, and I'm sorry I put you in this position."

Heather shrugged. "It's okay, I guess." She reached for the syrup and drowned her pancakes. "Grandma Connor said I should get a tattoo."

It took Darcie a moment to catch up with the subject switch. "Your dad would have a fit. Don't listen to Grandma Connor."

A slow grin spread across Heather's face. "You've got one."

"That's—"

"One what?" Flynn asked, coming back into the room and sitting down next to Darcie.

"A tattoo," Heather said, the light of good-natured challenge in her blue eyes.

"Don't even think about it, kiddo. In this case, I'm going to insist you do as I say and not as Darcie does."

Grandma Connor gave an unladylike snort, causing Heather to giggle. "Don't be a fuddy-duddy. You ought to lighten up and get one yourself. Or how about a pierced ear? You'd look good with a diamond just there in the left one." She pointed with her fork, dribbling syrup on the starched tablecloth.

"What, are you into pain or something this morning?" Flynn asked. "Tattoos and piercings hurt." He looked back at Heather. "They hurt *really* bad. And you know how you are with needles."

A phone rang and he frowned when everyone in the kitchen went utterly still. Grandma Connor glanced under the kitchen table.

"Darcie, your purse is ringing," she said helpfully.

"Thanks, Grandma." She retrieved her purse and fished for the phone, flipping it open and putting it to her ear.

Rose, Johnny and Grandma Connor still appeared to be holding their breath. Darcie's face underwent a transformation that ran the gamut of emotions in a split second. She met her mother's eye, nodded and stood, leaving the room.

"It's her hot line," Rose explained, staring pensively at the doorway through which her daughter had disappeared. "There must be a child in trouble."

"I thought she had to be at the hot line place to take the calls," Heather said, then colored and made a point of not meeting Flynn's eyes.

The reminder that Heather had called that hot line threatening to run away gave Flynn a punch in the gut. He'd do anything to keep his family safe and couldn't even think about the possibility of losing his daughter.

"Usually she *is* at the office. But some kids call more than once, and they ask for Darcie personally. When that happens, the volunteers transfer the call directly to Darcie's cell phone. She's easy to talk to, and she will always drop everything for them." Rose gave Heather a long look. "You can count on her."

The air in the room was thick with worry, and Flynn imagined that it would remain that way until Darcie came back to give a report.

He wondered how she handled it, day in and day out. This was more than a hot line to Darcie, more than a volunteer service. He knew that each call she took was her friend Tammy all over again. And the pressure she put on herself in her need to atone was enormous.

"I hope the kid is okay," Heather said, her voice sounding very young.

"I'm sure he or she will be," Rose said. "Darcie will see to it. You watch."

Flynn scooted his chair closer to Heather and put his arm around her, feeling his insides clutch as she laid her head on his shoulder.

He considered himself lucky that it had been Darcie who'd taken Heather's call. Although she wouldn't discuss their conversations, he credited her with soothing Heather's emotions, of convincing her to stay.

Now, if she would just have a little faith in her

powers of persuasion, she would realize that their cloud *did* have a silver lining. And that although Heather had her ups and downs, she was a loving child who would accept Darcie into the family.

Wouldn't she?

Oh, God, that tiny seed of uncertainty scared the hell out of him. He wanted to believe that all was well.

But what if it wasn't?

Mary Beth leaned sideways in the wood high chair that the Morettis kept for when their grandchildren visited, her little hand reaching as though she understood that emotions were shaky. Flynn tugged the chair closer and put his other arm around the baby.

She patted his face with a sticky hand, then treated Heather to the same affection. For once Heather didn't make a peep, and a horrible desperation built in Flynn's gut. He couldn't read his daughter's mind and in the worst way, he wanted to.

A sense of impending doom swamped him for no reason at all. He couldn't put his finger on what the problem was.

But he felt as though his world was about to come crashing down around his ears. It was probably just the reminder of the hot line, the reminder that his own daughter had been on the other end of one of those phone calls that Darcie was so good at handling. Situations he couldn't come close to managing.

His arms tightened around his girls.

At all costs, he couldn't allow anything to happen to his family.

He would keep his girls safe. He would keep them with him. He would master his skills as a dad—for these two children as well as the one who would be born in three months' time.

He shook off the antsy feeling, kissed each of his daughters on the head.

And, he told himself, he would convince Darcie Moretti to marry him.

Chapter Thirteen

The house was quiet for once, with Darcie and Mary Beth both napping, and Heather holed up in her room doing who knows what. Probably had the phone glued to her ear.

He ought to take advantage of the lull and get some work done, but as he moved toward his drafting table, the doorbell rang.

Heather came thundering down the stairs, ice skates swinging by their laces. She opened the door, and Flynn's eyes widened.

Four girls and two boys stood on his front steps, all dressed for outdoors.

"Hi, guys," Heather said, starting to step outside with her friends.

"Heather," Flynn called. When she glanced back at him, he raised his brows. "Can I see you for a minute?"

She gave a long-suffering sigh, told her friends she'd be right out and pushed the door shut. "What?"

"What's going on here?"

"We're gonna ice-skate on the pond."

"You might have told me you'd invited friends over." It was late in the afternoon. Close to suppertime. Would they expect a meal? Hell, it was hard enough cooking for four. He didn't think he could handle ten. Besides, he'd only thawed four pork chops. That could prove embarrassing, especially since he knew Liz's mother never hesitated to invite Heather to stay if she happened to be there.

"We'll be right outside," Heather said. "What's the big deal? I didn't think I needed to ask permission to hang out in my own yard."

"There's no need to make a federal case out of a simple question, Heather."

"Well, that's what you're doing, isn't it?"

He ran a hand over his face, feeling a hundred years old. Heather lost her militant stance, as though she understood he was darn near pushed to his Mr. Mom capability limits.

"We'll be right outside at the pond, Daddy. It's frozen solid. You checked it yourself just the other day, remember? You said we could use it."

Yeah, but he hadn't expected a party. He nodded.

"Can I go now?"

He waved her out the door. "Go."

Turning, he looked at his computer, sighed and made his way to the kitchen. Through the window over the sink he could see the kids gliding across the frozen pond, stocking caps pulled low over their ears, scarves flapping in the breeze, gloved hands shoving, poking and grabbing amid gay laughter.

Oh, he couldn't hear the sounds, but he could see the happiness of youth on their faces.

And Heather was right. He was making a big deal over nothing. At least she was hanging out at home rather than someplace else where there might be trouble. This way he could keep an eye out. Maybe even use the opportunity to bond. Bone up on his male domestic skills even.

To that end, he opened the refrigerator and took out a plastic container of milk, pouring the whole gallon in a huge saucepan and adding a generous amount of cocoa. The kids would be cold from ice skating, and nobody in their right mind would turn down hot chocolate.

He turned the burner on high, figuring the milk was ice cold and it would take a hot flame to get it going. Maybe he should make some cookies to go with it. He had a package of the kind that you slice. That shouldn't be too hard.

He read the directions on the package, flicked on the oven to the proper temperature. Fifteen minutes should do it. No sweat.

And if the group ended up staying, he'd order out for pizza.

DARCIE HEARD THE SOUND of teenage laughter and looked out the upstairs window. Heather and her friends were clowning around, skating backward and forward and in figure eights. The sight made her smile.

This was what Heather needed. Good friends to hang out with. The opportunity to do youthful things, to not have to think about adult responsibilities and hurts, real or perceived.

The grounds around Flynn's house were enormous, with a forestlike stand of trees bordering the yard. Snow clung to the ground and the branches of the pines. A bright red cardinal perched on the balcony railing, a crimson splash of color against the stark white snow.

She heard Mary Beth talking gibberish to one of her stuffed animals in her crib and went to get her. Mary Beth looked up, her sweet face breaking into a cherub smile, her pudgy arms reaching up.

"Da-Da," she squealed.

Darcie laughed. "Close, sweetie babe. Say Darcie, not Da-Da." *Or say Mama.* Oh, what she wouldn't give to be these children's mother.

She changed Mary Beth's diaper and carried her downstairs, surprised by the smell of baking cookies.

She stopped in the doorway of the kitchen. "I thought you were working," she said.

Flynn whirled around. His handsome features softened when he saw them in the doorway. "Six kids showed up at the door for an impromptu skating party. I figured that was more important than blueprints." He leaned against the counter, his hands covered with oven mitts. "And I thought you were resting."

Her face colored. They both knew why she needed to rest. She'd gotten very little sleep last night. But, it was worth it. "The smell of chocolate chips will get to me every time. Pulled me right down the stairs.''

Casually she moved to the stove and lowered the flame under the bubbling cocoa. No doubt it would be stuck to the bottom of the pan.

Flynn took the cookies out of the oven and set them on the counter to cool a bit. Removing the hot pads from his hands, he stepped next to Darcie, brushing back the wildly curling tendrils of hair from her temples. Her skin was so soft, slightly flushed from sleep or the steam of the hot milk. He wasn't sure. Or maybe it was from the reminder of their night together.

He pressed his lips to her hair, then untangled Mary Beth's fingers from his own hair. ''Ouch, baby. You'll snatch Daddy bald.''

Mary Beth clapped and giggled.

''So, what are you planning here? Are you going to invite everyone in for hot chocolate?''

He shrugged. ''Actually, I thought maybe I'd take it out to them.'' He wanted his daughter to realize that he cared. He wanted to impress those kids, make it so they'd go back to school tomorrow and brag about Heather O'Grady's dad doing something really cool.

Darcie smiled at him as though she realized what was on his mind. ''In that case, you'll need some help carrying the stuff out. Give me a minute to bundle up Mary Beth, and I'll give you a hand.''

Emotions swelled inside of him. The words *I love you* were on the tip of his tongue. But she struck up a nonsense conversation with the baby and left the room in search of coats and hats.

There would be time for declarations later.

One thing was for sure, though. This was starting to feel just like a real family.

HEATHER WISHED she didn't have to go to school today. Yesterday had been so cool with all her friends coming over. At first she'd thought it was kind of corny that her dad had come out with hot chocolate and cookies, but Shane and Ryan had been totally impressed. And her girlfriends had thought Dad was a babe.

She normally didn't like to admit stuff like that, but it was true. Her dad was like one of those models in the magazines. And he looked really young.

She watched him crack eggs in the skillet. He was different lately. Happier. Always looking at Darcie with those soft looks. And Darcie looked at her dad that way, too.

It was fun when they all got together in the kitchen like this. But could she trust it to last? It had been sort of like this for the last couple of months that her mom had been pregnant with Mary Beth.

But when the baby had been born, it had all changed.

Heather glanced at Darcie's stomach. She was getting bigger around the middle. Something stung around Heather's heart, and she didn't understand what she was feeling. She wasn't really mad, or sad.

She was scared. In her experience, people who

had babies abandoned their families. Still, she missed her mom something fierce.

Darcie's cell phone rang, and they all tensed. Heather held her breath. But when Darcie started talking it didn't sound like she was counseling a kid from the hot line.

Unabashed, she listened to half of the conversation, her stomach growing tight, the smell of the breakfast cooking making her feel sick.

"Well, yes, I'm still interested in changing positions," Darcie said.

Tears stung the back of Heather's eyes and she glanced over at her dad. He, too, had stopped cooking and was listening, watching Darcie with one of those looks he always got when he was disappointed or upset.

"Yes." Darcie's smile was excited. "I understand. Let me get back to you on that." She hung up the phone and gave a little laugh. "Well," she said. "I'd almost forgotten about sending that company a résumé. I had the interview months ago."

"What company is that?" Flynn asked.

"Philadelphia Life. Very prestigious. Huge salary. They just called to offer me a job."

Flynn felt a sense of déjà vu and fought it. She hadn't accepted the job. And it was feasible to commute to Philadelphia—depending on what part. He didn't want to jump the gun, but his insides were twisting.

"I hadn't realized you were looking to change jobs."

"I've had feelers out. With the baby coming, I needed a better salary."

Heather jumped up from the table. "I gotta get dressed for school."

"What about breakfast?" Flynn asked, gesturing to the pan of eggs.

"You took too long. The bus will be here if I have to wait around for you to finish."

He frowned at the bite in her tone and the way she flounced out of the room. "Who put a bee in her pajamas?"

Darcie shrugged. "We are running a bit late this morning. Here, let me help you finish up. We can at least give her some toast to go."

He wanted to say to hell with the breakfast and just grab her to him and hold on. He wouldn't stand in the way of Darcie's happiness if this job was what she wanted. But, damn it, careers that involved a commute were tough on a relationship.

And he still hadn't gotten Darcie to commit to marriage. She would talk about him forming a bond with their child she carried, but she wouldn't discuss permanence between the two of them.

He glanced at the clock, surprised by how late it actually was. Moving to the kitchen doorway, he shouted up the stairs. "Heather! Get a move on. You're going to miss the bus."

A door slammed upstairs.

Heather ran down the stairs and dashed through the foyer, heading for the front door.

"Hold it right there, young lady."

She came to a halt, turned slowly, guiltily, and

then gave him a belligerent look. Flynn exhaled, counted to ten, and still the roiling in his gut didn't settle. They had been doing so well.

"Back upstairs you go and wash off that clown makeup."

"It's not clown makeup. God, I can't believe you said that to me. You might as well just tell me I'm ugly!"

"Give me a break, Heather. You know better than that. But you're thirteen, for God's sake. You've got enough black goop on your lids to color ten faces. And it's twenty degrees outside. There's no excuse for you parading around with your butt and your boobs hanging out." When the hell had she gotten so big? If he wasn't mistaken, she was wearing one of those push-up bras and she was practically falling out of her top.

She gave him a low-throated scream of frustration and turned her back on him, reaching for the door-knob. By damn, she was going to deliberately defy him! What next?

He glanced at the back of her white skirt and nearly came unglued. "When the hell did you start wearing G-string underwear? My God, Heather, I can see right through your skirt!" Marching across the foyer, he turned her by the shoulders and pointed her back toward the stairs. "Go change."

"Why do you even care what I look like?" she cried. "All you think about is Mary Beth and Darcie and that new baby." She looked past him, and Flynn turned, seeing Darcie in the doorway, her features pale.

He sent her an apology with his gaze. "Heather, I don't know what you're trying to pull here, but your attitude stinks."

"Yeah, well so does yours."

"I'm entitled. I'm the parent. Now do as I say and go wash your face and change. I'll drive you to school if I have to."

She wrenched away from him and raced up the stairs. He could hear shoes hit the wall, and he winced. She wasn't gone but two minutes before she reappeared on the stairs wearing wrinkled jeans and a thick sweater. Mascara stained her cheeks and circled her eyes like a raccoon.

She brushed by him and yanked open the door. "I hope you're happy now. And I hope you know I hate you!" she screamed, glaring at both him and Darcie before running out the door and down the driveway toward the bus stop.

For a minute he was simply too stunned to move. Then he took a step, intending to go after her. It felt as though his brain was in a fog and bells were ringing in his ears. After a second, he realized it was Mary Beth's cries he was hearing.

"Flynn, let her go," Darcie said.

He paused, hung his head. "Where the hell did I go wrong?"

"You didn't." Darcie felt as though her heart was going to break in two. She understood better than anyone what had just gone on here. The job offer Flynn and Heather had overheard had brought back memories of Marsha, had opened wounds that would take much longer to heal.

She had no intention of accepting the job offer. Her family was here. Flynn and his daughters were here. The hot line was here.

And it was here that she wanted to be when she had her baby.

But Heather's expression had spoken much louder than words. And the between-the-lines feelings had fairly shouted.

It was over. Darcie had held out hope that Heather was coming to accept her, to accept them as a family.

But it wasn't to be. And the display they'd just witnessed proved how fragile and volatile the situation was.

Is this how Tammy had felt when her dad had brought Glenda home? Had she felt shut out? Out of control? Without a say or a choice? Forced into a situation she couldn't tolerate because she was a kid?

Had Tammy's father all those years ago echoed what Flynn had just said? *I'm entitled. I'm the parent. Do as I say.*

"Darcie?" Flynn brushed her arm, gave a squeeze.

She passed Mary Beth into his arms and stepped back.

He frowned and, oddly enough, she noticed that his hands were shaking, that a pulse was beating in his temple.

"You know, don't you?" she whispered.

"Don't say it."

"I have to, Flynn. I have to leave."

"No."

"Yes. We've known from the beginning this might happen."

"She was just throwing a tantrum. She's done this before. She'll come around."

"Maybe. Maybe not. I'm not willing to take the chance, and if you're honest with yourself, you'll admit that you aren't, either. Our relationship isn't good for your daughter, Flynn. At least not right now it isn't."

"But you're having my baby!"

She looked up at the ceiling, swallowed, refused to let her tears fall. If she did, she might never stop. She had to be strong. She had to make him see that this was best.

"I've told you before, Flynn. We can't sacrifice one child for another. Heather needs you now. She needs stability and to know that you value her needs and opinions. You can't just tell her you're bringing another woman into her life, a woman who would be replacing her mom."

"Her mom's been gone for over a year. She walked out long before she died. It's not like I'm rushing things."

"Maybe it doesn't feel that way to you. But to Heather, life's rocky curves are more than she can handle."

He blanched and she could see that her words were conjuring up all sorts of scary scenarios. Good. This was serious.

"My friend Tammy cried out to be heard...." She paused, drew in a breath as well as her composure.

"None of us was listening. I won't make that mistake again." She moved toward the stairs, wrapped her fingers around the smooth wood of the banister. "Hear Heather's cries, Flynn. Let her know that she's important, that she matters in your life. That she comes first."

"I'm trying, Darcie. But in the meantime what about us?"

She put her fingers over his lips, felt her own tremble. She could hardly get any words past her throat. "Don't make it any harder, Flynn. You can't change my mind."

Mary Beth leaned forward in Flynn's arms, her tiny hands opening and closing in a gesture that meant she wanted Darcie to take her. "Da-cee."

Tears flooded her throat, choking her. She tried for a smile, wrapped her hand around Mary Beth's pudgy wrist, kissed her drool-slick fingers.

Instead of going upstairs to pack, she stretched on tiptoe and pressed a kiss to Flynn's mouth, then hooked her coat off the hall tree and grabbed up her computer and purse and let herself out the door.

Her heart and throat were stinging something fierce.

For the sake of a teen, Darcie would sacrifice anything.

Including the love of her life.

The father of her baby.

Chapter Fourteen

Darcie couldn't remember a time when she'd hurt so badly. She should have never gotten involved with Flynn and his family—she'd known it was a mistake. Known that her heart would get broken.

She'd allowed herself to hope, lulled them all into a false sense of security. She should have known better.

And now look. Here she was a week later, still at her parents' house, still an emotional mess but doing her best to hide it. She'd lived the fairy tale for a while, burying her head against reality, and she hadn't looked for a new place to live.

A tiny part of her had believed that if she wished so hard for something it was bound to be hers. Pitiful that a thirty-one-year-old woman should kid herself so.

She'd dedicated her life to the teens. Promised Tammy all those years ago, while the mound of dirt was still fresh over her best friend's grave, that she would never ignore the hurt of another teen. She would always be in tune to the cry and never, ever assume it was a false one.

No matter how many times a kid might cry wolf, Darcie would listen and heed; she would put her own needs aside.

"Forgive me, Tammy," she whispered, feeling the punch of pain even after all these years.

She leaned against the wall, gazing out the front picture window, not really seeing anything. Late-afternoon sunlight streamed through the plate glass, bathing her face, coloring the world outside with buttery hope.

But not for Darcie. Because she knew that if she opened the door, the snap of frigid air would be there to suck away the warmth, a pessimistic breeze that blew through the heart and warned of the peril of wishing for too much.

Feet on the ground, Darcie.

"Well, aren't you a sight."

Darcie glanced at her mother, tried for a smile.

"You act so brave, but it's all bottled up inside you. That's not good for the baby, Darcie."

"I'm fine, Ma."

Rose shook her head, wiped her hands on the dish towel she held. "I don't understand you. You have a man willing and *wanting* to be a father to his child, yet you deny him and yourself and hide here at your mother's house. I didn't raise a coward, Darcie."

"I'm not—"

"You've loved Flynn O'Grady since you were a girl, and don't try to tell me different."

Darcie bit her lips, the emotions coming so fast

and so hard she couldn't seem to field them or find a slot for them.

"You thought I didn't see his name written all over the grocery sack covers of your schoolbooks? The puppy love? The sadness when he married? You stood back and let everyone else have a piece of him and never asked for yourself. And now you're doing the same."

"Ma, this has to do with his *daughter*."

"And the one in your womb, too. Don't forget about her."

"I'm not. But I can take care of her on my own, shield her from wounds before they can form."

Rose flapped her hands in a gesture of frustration. "You're being ridiculous!"

Oh, if only she could believe that she was. "You just don't get it, Ma." How could she explain? "Pretend you and Daddy weren't together—"

"Nonsense," Rose interrupted, shaking her head as though the very thought would bring bad karma down on all their heads.

"Pretend," Darcie pleaded.

"Fine." Rose flapped her hands again. "I'm pretending."

"Fine," Darcie echoed her mother's tone, making an effort not to shout. "So you start dating, but you've got me and Johnny and Celia to care for. But you fall for this man...."

Rose shook her head as though this was a ridiculous waste of time.

Darcie glared. "You fall for this man," she repeated, "but me and Celia and Johnny *hate* him."

"Heather does not hate you."

Darcie nearly screamed. "Think, Ma. Picture it with us—you, me, Johnny and Celia. You're a great mom and you've always put us first."

"Of course. That's my job, and I love you."

"But what if Daddy wasn't our dad? And you wanted him." She figured she'd have better luck if she painted her father in the role of the man. Rose had only loved one man in her life, and that was Johnny. Like mother like daughter, Darcie thought, for she too had only loved one man.

Flynn O'Grady.

"What if you wanted Daddy more than life itself, but *we* didn't want him? We're too young to be on our own. We're your responsibility. You love us. Who do you choose?"

"Oh, Darcie...."

"Who do you choose, Ma?"

"My children," she whispered.

"Yes."

Rose opened her arms and Darcie stepped into them. Grandma Connor came around the corner, stopped, and for once didn't make any wisecracks. Her wrinkled eyelids slanted at the corners where moisture pooled.

Darcie's cell phone, resting on the hall table, shrilled.

With a sickening sense of dread, a sixth sense that tracked eerie chills down her spin, Darcie reached for the phone.

And she knew before she ever heard the first trembling word.

"Darcie? I'm scared."

Oh, God. "Heather? Sweetie, where are you?" It was hard to keep her voice steady, to sound calm. She wanted to scream, to run. She could hear music in the background, a man's voice. Or maybe a boy's. It was hard to tell.

"Grandma Rose said you'd always come. I didn't mean what I said—" She broke off, crying.

Darcie was scared out of her mind. Her heart pounded so hard, it made it difficult to speak, to hear.

But it was so important that she hear.

Somebody pounded on the front door causing Darcie to nearly jump out of her skin.

"Sweetie, calm down. Tell me where you are. Give me an address and I'll be right there." It wasn't a question of *if* she should come. That was the mistake she'd made with Tammy.

This was Darcie's worse nightmare. Losing a kid. That it was Flynn's kid, a girl she loved like her own, nearly brought her to her knees.

With the phone hooked between her shoulder and ear, she snatched up pen and paper and yanked open the door.

Flynn and Mary Beth stood on the front porch.

She fought the dizziness brought on by the fierce surge of adrenaline. Elation mingled with fear and uncertainty.

He looked distraught, yet his immediate concern for her showed without question. It was there in the darkening of his eyes, the paling of his skin, the swift, sure brace of his hand as he slipped his arm around her waist, silently telling her he was here for her, that he would catch her if she fell, hold her if she cried, pick her up if she needed.

He had no idea it was Heather she was talking to. He'd set aside his own parental terror to bolster her.

If she'd had doubts before, she didn't now. This man loved her.

His gaze was her lifeline.

The fact that his daughter had called was her hope.

She adjusted the receiver. "I'm ready, honey. Give me an address."

"I don't know it." Heather was starting to cry harder. "I just need to get out of here."

"Are you in danger?" She wanted to tell her to hang up and call the police, but for her own peace of mind, she needed to know where Heather was so she could go to her.

"No. Robbie brought me to this house, and there's a bunch of guys here and some girls, too, and they're drinking and...I don't want to be here. The house is close to the park. Can you come get me there?"

"Is it safe for you to leave? To walk alone?" It was the middle of the day and the teens were having a drinking party?

"Yeah," she sniffed. "I'll be okay. They're wasted and probably won't even see me leave."

"Can you trust Robbie to walk with you?"

Flynn stiffened beside her, jerked back, his eyes going black. He'd just caught on to whom she was talking to. Emotions shifted across his face like gray clouds streaking over the face of the sun.

She knew he wanted to snatch the phone from her. That he didn't said a lot about his trust in her. He settled, though he still looked shaken. He cupped her neck, massaged the tension in her shoulders, encouraged and supported.

Trusted her enough to put the possible fate of his daughter in her hands.

The image of Tammy's grave, fresh dirt mounded amidst grass and sprays of roses and carnations flashed across her mind.

"I don't want Robbie to go anywhere with me. He doesn't..." Heather's voice had dropped to a whisper and Darcie didn't know if it was fear or sadness.

"Okay. Listen to me, Heather. You leave right now. Do you hear me? Go straight to the park and I'll be there. Don't you leave that park until I get there. You watch for me. It'll take me ten minutes tops. Don't get in anybody's car, okay?"

"Okay."

"Promise."

"I promise." The phone disconnected.

"I know where she is." Darcie shoved her arms through the sleeves of her coat.

"She's with Robbie Sanders?" Flynn asked, picking up Darcie's purse and draping it over her arm.

"Not *with* him. I don't know the story. I just know I need to get to her."

"Johnny!" Rose called, taking off her apron. "Get the car."

"Ma, no."

"Don't even try to stop me. This is pure nonsense what you kids are doing to yourselves. We're going and that's that. Heather should know that she has family to support her."

"Thank you, Rose," Flynn said, passing Mary Beth into her grandmotherly arms when she held them out. He looked at Darcie. "Your mother's right. I love you, Darcie Moretti, and we're going to find a compromise."

The car keys cut into her palm when she clenched her fingers into a fist. "Heather has to come first."

He put his hands on her shoulders. "Hawkins Park is open and in a good neighborhood." He squeezed her shoulders. "Heather isn't Tammy, Darc." He uncurled her fingers from around the keys and took them from her. "I'll drive."

"No. I told her *I* was coming. I don't want her to feel betrayed right off the bat by seeing your car."

"Then we'll take yours."

She held her hand out for the keys. "I need to drive, Flynn. I have to be in control. I can't explain it, but...I need to drive."

He nodded, and handed her back the keys. "Whatever you need," he said softly. "I'll always try to give it."

HEATHER SAT in the swing, the chain icy against her palm. It was getting cold out, but it wasn't dark yet.

Clouds had chased away the sun and threatened rain, but that wouldn't matter. Heather's sleeves were already wet from wiping her nose and her eyes.

She looked up and saw Darcie's blue Honda. And right behind it was Grandma Rose's white sedan. Technically Rose wasn't really her grandma, but it felt as if she was.

Heather wanted her to be.

She saw her dad get out of Darcie's car, and her heart bumped against her ribs. She didn't want to face him. He'd been so sad lately. And it was her fault.

She wanted to disappear, but Darcie was coming to her, nearly running, and Heather found her own feet moving, picking up speed, carrying her right toward those open arms.

The baby in Darcie's stomach bumped against her as Darcie squeezed. It made Heather cry even harder.

"I don't want to run away! And I don't want you to go away! I'm sorry."

"Shh, honey. You're safe. That's all that matters right now." Darcie was stroking the girl's back.

It was just the kind of motherly fussing that Heather craved. She tried not to be such a baby, tried to quit crying.

"How did you pick up my dad so fast?" Her breath hiccuped.

"I didn't. He showed up at my parents' house right when you called. The school told him you'd skipped today. He was frantic, Heather, and so was I."

Heather looked over Darcie's shoulder, noticed that Grandma Connor, Johnny and Rose—holding Mary Beth—were walking toward them. She felt embarrassed because they all knew she'd tried to run away.

"I didn't mean to be such a brat," she said, sniffing. She glanced down at Darcie's stomach. "That's not true. I did it on purpose because I got scared. Every day I kept worrying that I was gonna mess up and do something bad that would cause you to leave—like my mom did."

"Oh, Heather." Darcie held her, rocked her, hugged the confused, wounded girl's slight body to hers.

"And when you got the job offer...I didn't want you to leave, but I knew you would, so I pretended I hated you and that I wanted you gone because I figured it wouldn't hurt as bad if it was my choice. But I was wrong. It hurts real bad. And my dad's been so sad. It's all my fault. I didn't mean to make you not love him anymore."

"Oh, hon, you couldn't make that happen. I've loved your dad since I was a young girl—about your age." She wondered if Flynn could hear. He stood a few paces back, giving her the trust and space she'd asked for.

"Really?"

"Really. But he didn't even know I was alive. Still, I built my dreams around him. And then through the society pages of the paper, I watched him court your mom and then marry her."

"Did it make you sad?"

"Yes." She smiled apologetically. "At the time it did. But I'm not sorry he married her. Your mom was a beautiful woman. And she had you."

"But she left."

"That wasn't your fault. And it didn't diminish her love for you. Always believe that, Heather. She needed to do something for herself. That didn't have anything to do with you." She sent up a silent prayer that her words were true.

"It still made me feel bad."

"I know. But you're so lucky to have your dad. He's always been there. No matter what. You know I'm right, don't you?"

Darcie held her by the shoulders, an arm's length separating them, but in her palms were warmth and safety, and in her eyes was love.

Heather glanced at her father and nodded, fresh tears spiking her lashes, mascara running like black ribbons over her cheeks and chin.

"He's your rock, Heather."

Darcie moved aside, her own throat working as Flynn opened his arms and his daughter slipped into them, burying her face against his chest.

"I'm sorry, Daddy."

"I know, baby." He kissed her hair. "I love you. But we're going to stop all this nonsense. We've been through some rough patches since your mom's accident. And a lot of that is my fault. I've been so afraid of losing you, of failing as a father, that I've been walking around on eggshells and sacrificing in ways that aren't fair to any of us."

He pushed his daughter's silky hair off her brow,

pressed his lips there and held her against his heart. Later they would talk about what happened here today, where she had been. Not now.

"No more, kiddo. Look around you. Love is strong. And family is strong. Look at how many arms are just waiting to hold you, to love you. And they're not even officially family yet."

"Yet?" Heather asked, her watery smile spreading, acceptance and relief shifting across her features.

"Yet. We're going to work together to make this a real family. And that includes Darcie and the new baby, too."

"Yeah. I want that." She sniffed.

Flynn tipped up her chin, looked directly into her liquid blue eyes, making sure he had her full attention. "I'm not going anywhere, Heather. And neither are you. Got that?"

She nodded.

He looked over at Darcie. "Ditto that to you, too."

Grandma Connor gave a war whoop, startling them all. "Be still my heart." She held out a hand, beckoning. "Heather, let's you and me talk about piercing these old ears of mine. I've a mind to get me some rubies to go with this red hairdo."

Heather giggled and kissed her dad. "Darcie's looking kind of stubborn, Daddy." She raised her voice. "And really, Daddy, you're not being a very good influence on me and Mary Beth. I mean, Darcie's gonna give us a sister in a few months, and you guys aren't even married. You better do something about that.''

Darcie's heart pounded so hard, she wondered if she would faint. The look on Flynn's face when he glanced her way made her tremble all over.

''Yeah, I'd better,'' he said and strode toward her, determination radiating, a sexy half smile pulling at his lips.

Darcie glanced around. They had an audience. Her parents, her grandmother, his kids.

She retreated a pace.

His smile widened and he winked. ''You can think about running, but I guarantee you I'm faster.'' He wrapped an arm around her waist, pulled her right up against him and crushed his lips to hers.

The power of the kiss whipped through her, blanking her mind, washing her in sensation and love.

His lips gentled, yet hers clung. He smiled against her mouth, slid his hand from her back to frame her pregnant belly. When she looked up, his chocolate eyes had softened with such profound reverence her throat ached.

''Marry me,'' he said, his voice low and sandpaper rough.

''Why?''

The sexy curve of his lips told her he already knew he was the victor. ''Because you've loved me since you were a girl of thirteen. You said so.''

She tried to keep the smile from her face. ''And?''

''Because I love you. I might have been blind all

those years ago, but not anymore." His voice went impossibly soft, trembled. "You are my heart, Darcie Moretti."

Tears flooded her eyes. It was absolutely ridiculous how she'd become such a watering pot of emotions lately.

"Sweetheart...?"

"Yes."

The baby kicked against his palm. His Adam's apple bobbed in his neck. "You'll marry me?"

"Oh, yes." She placed her hand over his—over *their* child. "We've already been told we're setting a bad example to our children."

Our children. He pulled her close, held her, took a minute to gather his emotions. He wasn't certain he could speak just yet.

He cleared his throat, lifted his head and looked at Heather who stood with the Morettis and Mary Beth. A grin spread across his face. They were giving a hell of a public display.

But that was okay. This was family.

He lifted his arm, inviting Heather to join them. "She said yes," he called.

Heather leaped, kissed Grandma Connor, danced Rose and Mary Beth in a circle, squeezed Johnny, and then ran to Flynn and Darcie, hugging and kissing. Then she stopped and frowned.

"This doesn't mean you're gonna give up your Wednesday night Daddy Club meetings, does it?"

Flynn felt a jolt and wondered if he was about to take a direct hit to his ego. "Why?"

Heather shrugged, trying to look casual. "I've

gotten kind of used to Ruth Naomi's classes. And you're doing pretty good in those bonding sessions with those other guys.''

''Is that a polite way of saying I've still got a lot to learn?''

Heather shrugged again—this time the gesture full of the devil—and cut her gaze to Darcie.

''Oh, that's right. Both of you gang up on me, why don't you?'' But there was no heat to his voice. Only love. And happiness unlike any he'd ever known.

He hadn't officially graduated from The Daddy Club, but he'd developed enough Mr. Mom skills to run the thing.

And that might not be a bad idea.

He looked down at Darcie, at the sexy freckles covering her face, her wide smile. ''You still going to be handing out financial advice to those KoffeeKlatch women?''

''Of course. I've a knack for it.''

He hooked one arm around Darcie's shoulders and the other around Heather's, steering them toward the Morettis. ''Then I guess I'll keep going to the meetings. Besides, those classes will come in handy when the next baby's born…and the next one after—''

''Daddy, please! Give Mom a chance to have this one first!''

Mom.

Darcie and Flynn stopped as though they'd slammed into an invisible wall.

Heather nearly spoiled the moment by crying. All

she'd ever wanted was love and security...and for the pain to go away. She wanted a family and a chance to be a kid—not a grown-up at thirteen.

But she'd been afraid to *be* that kid, afraid to be too needy. Because then her dad might go away, too.

She knew better now.

Her dad and Darcie had their arms wrapped around each other, but Heather didn't feel left out. She felt lucky.

"You *are* my rock, Daddy. And so is Darcie. It didn't matter if I was acting like a jerk or if she was mad at me or busy doing something else. She came to me when I got scared. She never made me feel wrong or bad or second best."

Heather looked at Darcie, spoke directly to her. "You always made me feel special and loved. Just like a mom. And I'm really lucky that you've chosen to be mine."

"And Mary Beth's," Darcie whispered, giving up the battle to stem her tears. "I love you guys. And I love your dad, too."

"Yeah, we're pretty easy to love—most of the time." Heather made a half turn. "But we better get this family gathered up and hit the road. Grandma Connor wants me to pierce her ears."

"Now wait a minute," Flynn said, but Heather had already skipped away. He looked down at Darcie and couldn't help but press his lips to hers. He would never get enough of her as long as he lived. "Your grandmother is a menace."

"Think so? Wait till she joins the KoffeeKlatch ladies at the hardware classes. You thought Marge and Ula Mae and Ruth Naomi had mouths. Grandma can run circles around them.''

Flynn smiled. ''I'm going to love being part of your family, Darcie Moretti-soon-to-be-O'Grady.''

''And I yours, Flynn O'Grady. It's what I've wanted for most of my life.''

Starting December 1999, a brand-new series about fatherhood from

 Three charming stories about dads and kids... and the women who make their families complete!

Available December 1999
FAMILY TO BE (#805)
by Linda Cajio

Available January 2000
A PREGNANCY AND A PROPOSAL (#809)
by Mindy Neff

Available February 2000
FOUR REASONS FOR FATHERHOOD (#813)
by Muriel Jensen

Available at your favorite retail outlet.

Come escape with Harlequin's new

Series Sampler

Four great full-length Harlequin novels bound together in one fabulous volume and at an unbelievable price.

Be transported back in time with a Harlequin Historical® novel, get caught up in a mystery with Intrigue®, be tempted by a hot, sizzling romance with Harlequin Temptation®, or just enjoy a down-home all-American read with American Romance®.

You won't be able to put this collection down!

On sale February 2000 at your favorite retail outlet.

HARLEQUIN®
Makes any time special ™

Visit us at www.romance.net

PHESC

3 Stories of Holiday Romance from three bestselling Harlequin® authors

Valentine Babies

by

ANNE STUART

TARA TAYLOR QUINN

JULE McBRIDE

Goddess in Waiting by Anne Stuart
Edward walks into Marika's funky maternity shop to pick up some things for his sister. He doesn't expect to assist in the delivery of a baby and fall for outrageous Marika.

Gabe's Special Delivery by Tara Taylor Quinn
On February 14, Gabe Stone finds a living, breathing valentine on his doorstep—his daughter. Her mother has given Gabe four hours to adjust to fatherhood, resolve custody and win back his ex-wife?

My Man Valentine by Jule McBride
Everyone knows Eloise Hunter and C. D. Valentine are in love. Except Eloise and C. D. Then, one of Eloise's baby-sitting clients leaves her with a baby to mind, and C. D. swings into protector mode.

VALENTINE BABIES

On sale January 2000 at your favorite retail outlet.

HARLEQUIN®
Makes any time special™

Visit us at www.romance.net   PHVALB

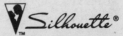

HEART OF THE WEST

Every Man Has His Price!

Lost Springs Ranch was famous for turning young mavericks into good men. So word that the ranch was in financial trouble sent a herd of loyal bachelors stampeding back to Wyoming to put themselves on the auction block!

July 1999	**Husband for Hire** Susan Wiggs	January 2000	**The Rancher and the Rich Girl** Heather MacAllister
August	**Courting Callie** Lynn Erickson	February	**Shane's Last Stand** Ruth Jean Dale
September	**Bachelor Father** Vicki Lewis Thompson	March	**A Baby by Chance** Cathy Gillen Thacker
October	**His Bodyguard** Muriel Jensen	April	**The Perfect Solution** Day Leclaire
November	**It Takes a Cowboy** Gina Wilkins	May	**Rent-a-Dad** Judy Christenberry
December	**Hitched by Christmas** Jule McBride	June	**Best Man in Wyoming** Margot Dalton

HARLEQUIN®
Makes any time special ™

Visit us at www.romance.net

PHHOWGEN